For The Rest Of My Life

Susan Marmo

LINDEN HILL PUBLISHING

Princess Anne, Maryland

www.lindenhill.net

For The Rest Of My Life

Susan Marmo

Limited First Edition

Printed in the United States of America

Linden Hill Publishing
11923 Somerset Avenue
Princess Anne, MD 21853

Copyright 2008

ISBN 978-0-9820153-0-8

Thank you!.......

My family and friends for their support, especially my father, Al Marmo

Maria Blake for knowing I'd have a sleepless night and having a great book waiting for me

K.S. Brooks for always having time for me

Nick Klepper for his words of encouragement

And my husband, Victor, for bringing all those nice, hot cups of tea to my desk.

TABLE OF CONTENTS

CHAPTER 1

"Oh, shit," Charlie said, frustrated, looking at the contents of her leather briefcase spilled on the hallway floor. "What day is it, Ally?" she snarled, rolling her eyes in disgust at her own clumsiness while grabbing for her blackberry, Mont Blanc pens, files, and day planner.

"Tuesday, Charlie, all day, it's been Tuesday," Allyson answered with a bit of sympathy for her stressed-out friend and colleague while handing over business cards, post-it notes and hand sanitizer she helped pick up.

"No, I mean the date!" Charlie snapped.

"The 17th?" Ally replied puzzled.

"I swear when I have PMS, I get so klutzy." Charlie sighed heavily in an attempt to compose herself.

"Well, if you didn't have so much crap in that briefcase, you might be able to close it properly," Ally added, "and things like this wouldn't happen. Slow down!"

"Slow down? You been talking to my father again? I hate it when he says that to me." Although Charlie was shaking her head, she knew Ally was right. "Ok, I am ready to roll."

"How much stuff do you need in a briefcase anyway? They could drop the bomb and you could live for a week I bet with the stuff you have in there, including a change of clothes!" Ally badgered her already aggravated friend.

"I like being prepared. Nothing wrong with that, is there? Hurry, we're gonna.... crap," Charlie announced as she saw the elevator doors close before her. The shiny doors revealed the reflection of a normally well-put together, confident person looking a bit out of sorts.

Charlie reached to smooth out her dark auburn hair and turned to check out her backside. *Is this pants suit getting tighter?*

"Re-lax Charlie!" Ally said all drawn out, "My God, you're freaking out. You can handle this; everyone knows you can. That's why you were chosen to go. You are always up for a challenge. Why is this so different for you?"

"When I am like this I don't cope well. I don't really know why, Ally. Wasn't I the one who always said I *can* do that, we *can* do that, no obstacle is too big etc, etc; I wonder too why this feels so overwhelming to me."

"What are you doing tonight?" Ally asked, trying to calm her friend by changing the subject, as they walked into the elevator.

"Packing I guess, with a touch of sulking, if I am lucky. You?" Charlie asked with a bit of sarcasm.

But knowing her friend, Ally knew there was probably some truth in what Charlie said. Over the past eight years, Ally had worked beneath Charlie as her administrative assistant. Charlie was one of her closest friends and the go-to gal for any issues in the large, high-stress office. Charlie was always poised and the voice of reason when things heated up. She was never at a loss for a creative solution to any problem. Ally had seen Charlie juggle catastrophe after catastrophe and make it look easy. Now to see her friend behaving so on edge made her think how she would have reacted to the news Charlie had received two weeks prior.

Charlie Watson had walked into work, as on any normal day, and was called into the CEO's office immediately. Mr. Moore informed her that in four weeks she was being sent to Edinburgh, Scotland to get the company's new acquisition up and running. The assignment was the first of its kind in the history of her company and was estimated to take a year to complete. Expenses and living arrangements were discussed, as well as job functions, company goals and other responsibilities. Charlie's life changed drastically in four hours.

The one thing Charlie knew about herself in the 32 years she had been alive was that she liked order. She required it. She was finally comfortable and happy with her life, which had required a series of events to come together in order for her to get there.

Charlie loved her job. It was thirteen miles away from her new house. She had total job security. A boss who not only respected her but relied heavily upon her. She had a terrific salary, great colleagues and stability.

She had finally bought the house of her dreams and now she couldn't wait for summer to plant her garden. All her family was finally back in Maryland within driving distance, so everyone could enjoy the holidays together. She had great friends with whom she regularly went out. She didn't want to be alone in a foreign country when all that she had hoped for here in Maryland was at long last fulfilled.

A month or two maybe, but a year to leave her house unattended, to not see her family or friends, nor be able to take her nieces and nephew to the beach for the Fourth of July, that was a lot to ask. It seemed too much of a sacrifice to walk away from the peace she had found in her routine and the contentment of her life.

How? How can you walk into work one day and be sent somewhere else for a year. And not just somewhere else like Idaho. No, no, no, nothing that simple for me, I have to get myself sent somewhere FOREIGN!

Self-pity was not an emotion with which Charlie was familiar. She was always graced with good fortune. Being prepared meant very few surprises, Charlie had learned. But this unexpected directive was a huge surprise.

She knew her job well. It came as second nature to her. *How do you teach someone something you just KNOW how to do?* she thought. Perhaps it was the uncertainty of this new plan that bothered her so much. She considered declining the offer, if it could even be considered an offer. However when she put the pros and cons on paper, as was her methodical way, there was only one thing for her to do - GO.

"Well, if you need any help, call me, bye" and with that Ally closed her car door.

Walking to her own car, Charlie found she was talking to herself, *I should be really excited. Who else gets an opportunity like this? I get a company credit card, a new apartment in a great downtown city. This could be an opportunity of a lifetime!*

CHAPTER 2

I can't believe it can rain this friggin' much in one country. How do these people do it! Charlie said under her breath as she hurried home to her new apartment from her first Saturday night out at a pub in Edinburgh. The wind was at the very least *blustery*, and the rain stung when it hit her bare hands. Her breath showed when she exhaled, reminding her she really did need to get in shape and go on a diet. All this walking she had done over the past two days since she arrived had to be helpful. *But the weather sucks! Not convenient for outdoor exercise at all.*

Putting her key in the street level door to enter the stairwell to her apartment, Charlie still couldn't get over how the apartments were on top of the shops. She was thankful she wasn't on top of a restaurant. She could only imagine the smells that would permeate her apartment. Climbing the stairs to her apartment, she was praising God again that she only had to go up one flight. Not only were the stairs well worn and narrow, but they were circular. She couldn't bear to think what it would be like to be up four or five more flights and having to carry groceries or children. *Heaven forbid you forget something.* But the first floor apartment was the only thing Charlie had been thankful for so far in her two days in Edinburgh.

Two days before, Charlie had been picked up in the morning at the airport by a taxi and delivered to an orange door. The driver had handed her the keys and helped her up the flight of steps with her bags. Trying to figure out the keys, Charlie turned to ask the driver which key was which for the two locks on the door but he had left! The company hadn't sent a representative to meet her nor a rental agent to assist her in directions. Nothing. No instructions. She was on her own to fend for herself. So she walked into her apartment all alone.

Wow, this is small, she muttered anxiously, not able to think in that moment what might be behind the three closed doors before her in the hallway.

The small foyer was barely big enough to close the door behind her once her bags were inside, but immediately made her choose from one of the three pine doors. *All that's missing is Monty Hall, s*he chuckled to herself. *I think I will pick Door Number Two.*

Leaving her bags, she pushed open the middle door. *The room is bigger than I would have thought.*

Before her was a living room/kitchen combination. The whole room was about 30 x 30 feet, nicely papered and decorated with a warm burnt orange and cream color scheme. Even the carpet matched impeccably. A window on the far wall looked onto what one would think at first to be a jungle. It appeared to be an over-grown play area but there were a few areas cleared for clotheslines. *How do you even get there?* she thought quickly, worried already about the ticks and bugs calling it home. *Hmm, no screen on the window either.*

Turning to face the kitchen area, she walked past a high bar ledge with green marble type Formica which, on the other side, opened to a work space for food preparation, a double sink, a very small stove with a built in oven, a dishwasher, and a microwave.

Where is the refrigerator? How the hell am I sup-pose to buy a refrigerator and where am I supposed to put it?! she whined.

There were ample white cabinets above the sink, and below the workspace there was large storage. But there was no furniture. No TV, no phone, no dishes, no couch, nothing. And it was cold. She walked back into the hall and went to Door #3. There was the bedroom. Not too small, a window again looking over the jungle, a small closet on the back wall and to her right were two sliding mirrored doors to a rather large closet, not deep but long. No bed, no cabinet for clothes. However, it too was decorated very tastefully in shades of rich blue and cream. The carpet seemed new and there was pine trim throughout.

Well, they didn't tell me I was going to have to furnish this place; that could take forever to find everything I need. On the bright side, it'll be a project to keep me busy. She chuckled to herself at this irony, *Like I'm going to need another project to keep me busy because the merger won't be enough.*

With one door left, she prayed it was a bathroom. And so it was a bathroom, small like the other rooms. There was a shower with a contraption like she'd never seen for the water to come out, no tub, a small sink with two faucets, one for the hot and one for the cold. *I didn't know that people did that anymore.*

No toilet paper.

Ok, Charlie, first things first. You need to go get some supplies and you can forget your nap 'cause there ain't nothing to sleep on or with, she said to herself mockingly.

It was 11 AM on a cold October Friday after Charlie had been up all night on a flight to a city she really didn't know much about. She started criticizing herself for not preparing and researching enough. She was apprehensive, and finally, being honest with herself, she was scared. There was no one to call to help her. There was no one to ask where to go to buy toilet paper and a Diet Coke. No one. She closed her eyes and leaned her head back slightly with one of those what-the-hell-have-

I-gotten-myself-into breaths. She looked around the odd shaped hallway with its deep red, shag carpet, and the three pine doors.

What the hell am I supposed to do now? she sulked. Reasoning with herself for a few short seconds, she sprang into action.

Stick with the plan, Lady. Grab your purse and keys and hit the road! You need to find toilet paper.

She set off down the steps, looking at her funny shaped keys, wondering if this country was still stuck in the 50's with their dual taps for hot and cold and keys that looked like her dad's from when he was a kid.

Stepping out on the wet sidewalk, she pulled her jacket tighter and made a mental note to buy an umbrella. There was a shop right next door that had vegetables and fruit sitting outside. Peering in, she saw candy, beer, a huge wall of wine behind the counter, and more vegetables. She walked in slowly, smiling politely at the Middle Eastern gentleman manning the counter.

"Hello, Miss, can I help you?"

He didn't have a Middle Eastern accent but rather a Scottish one. *Weird*, she thought.

"Thank you but I'm just looking around." *That's help, moron. Ask him where to go shopping.*

"Well, actually, I moved upstairs and I have never been here before and I need some groceries and a Cash Machine," she said sheepishly.

"The bank is down one block to the right, across the street on the corner. From here if you go left, up one block, again, on the other side of the street is the grocery store called the Scotmid. They will have what you need."

He must have recognized the look of relief on her face because he offered her a few words of encouragement, and said if she had any trouble she could come back and ask. He said he was open until 10 PM. They exchanged thank you's and she promised to be back to get her medicinal provisions, namely Ernest and Julio Gallo for her nerves. The shopkeeper laughed with her.

She headed to the bank first. She decided quickly to stick to the crosswalks, since she didn't want to get hit by a car so early on. She imagined it would take some time to get used to looking in the opposite direction before crossing. She was told that the office was nearby, within walking distance, and she gave a big 'thumbs-up' to that, as driving was definitely out of the question for awhile until she got accustomed to the opposite side of the road issue.

The bank was exactly where the gentleman had said it would be. She withdrew £200. The money was colorful and big.

How can it be that the money is big but everything else seems so small? Clydesdale Bank and The Bank of Scotland? How many places are allowed to make money here?

The Bank of Charlie sounded quite nice remembering all the furniture and appliances she was going to have to buy. Following her new friend's directions, she walked up two blocks and found the store.

Oh my God, look at these baskets. They are double-decker and so small.

Thinking again about how people would have to carry their groceries up flights of stairs, she made a vow to only get a few things.

Ok, I have no refrigerator so I'm limited to things that don't need to be kept cold, and toilet paper, she reminded herself.

Grabbing two baskets, she put them on their respective spots on her double-decker shopping cart. She skipped the vegetables, picked up some apples, passed on the dairy goods, and tried to find bread for peanut butter and jelly sandwiches. As Charlie took in all the strange labels and food names, she realized how much she took for granted when going to the grocery store at home. There, she could grab her large cart and fill it with whatever she wished and then load everything into her car. She could drive back home, into her garage, and walk 20 feet to put everything away in her kitchen. Not hard; easy and simple. This seemed more complicated. You can't go on a big, huge shopping trip alone because you can't carry all that much by yourself. And things like a gallon of milk weigh a ton! *Where am I going to put a fridge?*

Charlie ended up in the meat section and was amazed at how expensive the meat was. She overheard a lady telling her daughter that they would go across to the butcher for their meat, that it was better there. *A butcher? Who goes to a butcher? I've never seen a butcher in a separate shop. My local Giant grocery store always had great meat and the butcher worked right there.*

Charlie grabbed a few cans of Diet Coke and added them to her shopping cart and decided she better stop there and if necessary come back. She remembered the toilet paper and headed for the checkout. The lady checked her items and announced £22.46 as her total. She handed the lady £40 and waited for her change. The checkout lady was shooting her a bizarre look that made Charlie feel uneasy. Following her eyes, Charlie realized that her groceries were sitting down the conveyor belt.

"Do I bag the groceries?" Charlie asked embarrassed.

"Aye, the bags are at the end," the checkout lady answered grudgingly.

Charlie hurried to the end and frantically started placing bread, Diet Coke, and jelly into the plastic bags as fast as possible, realizing she was now holding up the line. When she finished, she had five bags, correction, five **heavy** bags. Gathering them up as best she could, she hurried out the door as fast as possible.

It's been a long time, Charlie, since you were the one who needed help and not the one giving help. Remember how this feels for Monday.

The plastic bags started to dig into her fingers. *I hardly got anything. How could it be five bags? How could it have cost £22? That's like 40 bucks. I hardly got anything.* After several stops to regain the color and feeling in her fingers, she made it the one block back to her apartment.

Charlie placed the groceries on the worktop, walked to the center of the floor, and sat down heavily to think. It was already 1:30 PM. *I need to get a bed and I want to take a shower. I wonder if there is a Walmart here. I have no towels or blankets. I need to call my boss about furnishings, I need to set up a bank account, I have no cooking utensils. I have no phone.* With her mind going a mile a minute, Charlie started to break down and the tears of frustration came.

How am I supposed to do this!!!!! How am I supposed to know? I have the rest of today and then the weekend to get my shit together...there is no way. I need help.

Still sniffling, she made the decision to take a shower to clear her head. Using her robe as a towel, she unpacked her toiletries and proceeded to the bathroom.

"Ok," she said, "This can't be too hard," as she looked over the device carefully.

A ring with blue fading to red - *That must be the temperature.* There was another dial with one raindrop on top and below it two raindrops.

I have no idea what that means, but we will go with two raindrops.

She pressed the 'on' button and nothing happened.

You have got to be joking! How hard can it be to take a shower?

Charlie tried every possible combination between the temperature gauge and the raindrops. Not one worked. Discouraged, she opted for a sponge bath in the sink; her hair would have to wait. Turning the hot tap on, she waited a minute for the hot water to come through. She waited and she waited.

Devastated, she thought, *This is definitely God punishing me for pre-marital sex. I cannot come up with any other reason for this, no reason at all, I mean how is it water can be such an issue in a country boasting so many lakes! A shower that won't come on and a tap with no hot water, unbelievable!*

Hanging her head, she thought, *Suck it up, Watson. It's gonna be a cold one.*

Feeling more hygienic but far from more optimistic, she dressed and set out with a clear mission to find blankets and a pillow. Grabbing her backpack for easy toting should she find a store, she hit the street.

"So this is Home Street."

She walked toward the busier road observing all the different shops and stores along the way. She popped into an electronics store and bought a small wall clock and an alarm clock. Hitting a bigger intersection she finally felt a small glimmer of hope when she saw many stores that might offer up her immediate needs. She found a wonderful store that had most of what she required. She bought two pillows, a mug, a dish, a bowl, some silverware and utensils, a small pot and pan, and a blanket. Her backpack was pushing at the seams, and her hands were full.

Ali's Cave, I will have to remember this place and come back. Thank God for Ali's Cave!

Heading back to her apartment yet again, her stomach let her know she was hungry. *I wonder what the food is like in these parts?*

16

She dropped her treasures in the middle of the living room and started to make a plan.

It's 4:00 PM, that's 11 AM back home; I need to call Mr. Moore to find out about these furnishings. How and where do I do that? I'll have to go back out. I have to put all this stuff away and somehow organize the things I brought with me from home.

She went back down to her friend in what she was now calling 'the Edinburgh 7-11'.

"Hi ya, remember me?" she smiled wide.

"Aye, my pal, how did you get on earlier?" he asked.

"Your directions were great, thank you, but I have another question. I passed some phone booths up the road, but all I have are bills; can you give me a bunch of change so I can call the States?"

"We sell phone cards that offer better rates than if you put in change, this one here is £5 and will give you over a hundred minutes"

Her new friend gave her directions on how to use the card, advised her that phone booths are called 'call boxes', and directed her to the call box at a closer location. She hit the phone to call her boss.

"Mr. Moore, it's Charlie. Good, I am fine. The flight was ok. Yes, the apartment is nice but not furnished, how do I handle that expense-wise?"

Once she had asked all her questions and was satisfied with all the answers, she went back to her apartment. *Thank God for company credit cards. Now I have to figure out where to buy it all.*

Getting settled back at her apartment, she unloaded her groceries. *A radio - a must for tomorrow.* Looking over the stove and oven, she opened the dishwasher.

That's the fridge?! Charlie was astounded! *It's so small. And here I was worrying about carrying a gallon of milk; it won't even fit. That's the freezer? It won't even hold an ice cube tray. This is ridiculous. How do these people live?!*

She stood there shaking her head in awe at how different everything seemed to be in just the few hours she had spent walking around.

She made a sandwich and went into the bedroom to prepare a makeshift bed on the floor.

Man it's cold, where's the heat? she mumbled, rubbing her hands together.

She looked on all the walls for a thermostat.

You have got to be kidding me, there is no heat?! How can you live in a country where the mean temperature is like 40 degrees and not have heat! Can this get any worse?

With a resigned glance down at her feet, she realized what she had said and in an instant she knew the answer as well.

Things can and probably will get worse.

Not a good thought for someone who is normally an optimist. She began unpacking and threw on a few extra layers of clothes while she was at it. After finishing, she decided more organization was needed. She put some water in the microwave to make a cup of instant coffee then sat on her blanket to make a list. The list included all the appliances she would need including a hair dryer, a couch and end table, more blankets, a phone with service somewhere, more dishes and silverware, a dresser, hangers, an iron and the list went on and on.

A phone book, that's what I need. That should tell me some places to go and where to get phone service.

After spending an hour making a very comprehensive list, she could barely keep her eyes open. The problem was, it was only 7 PM.

Adding a hammer and nails to the list so she could hang her clock, she went to 'bed'. It was cold, uncomfortable, and dark.

CHAPTER 3

I've gone to bed at 4 AM but very rarely have I gotten up willingly at this time and on a Saturday morning to boot! she mumbled, stirring her coffee. *I wonder how long this day is going to be.*

Having another unsuccessful crack at the shower, Charlie began boiling water in her pot and filled the sink. Washing her hair was tricky but it was done, time consuming but done. She headed for the 'call box' and the phone book.

I don't know where any of these places are. A taxi driver could take me anywhere! The Bed Shed, sounds good. Leith…. I wonder how far Leith is? But I'd better go to the bank first.

She walked to the corner, entered the bank and went to the customer service counter.

"How may I help?" asked the representative.

"Hello, I would like to open a bank account." Charlie said politely.

"You'll need to fill in this form. When you are through, let me know."

Charlie took a seat and began filling in the form. *Surname, I guess that's my last name. Address, employment verification, hmmm.*

"Miss, I am not sure how to complete this portion. You see my company bought another company here and I was sent for about the next year or so to help with the takeover but the legal name is changing." Charlie went on with the explanation.

After an hour she lost her mind!

"How can you not let me open an account, I have worked for the same company for eight years and have proof of my steady income. It shouldn't matter that I have no pay stubs from Edinburgh. I can get letters faxed in the next ten minutes!"

The manager came over and explained the protocol, and as it turned out, there was no way she was going to be able to get an account, not even a savings account, until she had two pay stubs.

HOW, how? How can it be like this?!

Getting used to nothing being easy, Charlie took a calming breath and went to her list. Her bed was next.

Snagging a taxi, armed with an address, she was off. Two hours later, with her bed selected, she handed over her company credit card.

"So when will it be delivered?" Charlie asked, excited and proud of her accomplishment.

"November 8th between 8 & 12," the salesman answered.

"What? That's almost two weeks away. I need the bed today or sooner than Nov 8th! Is it back ordered, can I chose another bed?"

"No, it takes 7-10 business days for us to receive it and today is Saturday. Then we have to get you on the delivery schedule and we deliver to Tollcross on Tuesdays and Fridays."

"I see," she said dejected, "Thank you, have a good day."

With that she walked out to the street. *I wonder if I could walk back from here.* Charlie headed back in the direction the cab came. *Two week's!*

Flagging a cab, she asked how much a ride would be to The Furniture Store - £18.

"Wow, that's steep."

The cabbie advised her about the buses she could take, but that was too overwhelming at the moment. She would need to find something more local.

This is beautiful! she observed, staring at Edinburgh Castle and taking in the hustle and bustle of a Saturday on Princes Street.

Wow! She was floored.

People see this everyday. How lucky are they? Unbelievable! I wish I had brought my camera. How do you get up there? What's that? Looking at the monument perched on the side of the road. *That's awesome.*

She had been so overwhelmed by the beauty of the city that she had failed to notice the stores. There were stores, lots of stores, a huge garden walk, buildings with architecture like she had never seen, and to her grateful surprise a big blue 'I' sign! *Information, now you're talking!*

The information center was more of a store loaded with touristy trinkets and a line of windows to book tours and shows, and there were brochures. She picked up one of each. She couldn't wait to sit and look through everything that Edinburgh had to offer. She highly doubted she was going to be bored here.

Asking a stranger how to get back to her apartment, she set out on her journey. She passed several stores then popped in to one to pick up another blanket and a blow dryer. She priced some furniture but it was really expensive. Expensed through her work or not, there had to be other more affordable options. She again found her favorite store so far, Ali's Cave. She bought her hammer and nails, an iron, and a few other things to make life a bit more bearable for the time being.

There has got to be a Scottish Walmart type store somewhere!

She made a mental note to ask someone at her work once she started on Monday. At the thought of starting work, her stomach twisted in anxiety for a brief moment. Her boss had prepared her well for what was to happen in the first few weeks, but she was nervous about how it was going to be accepted. Change always brings out the worst in people. After these past thirty or more hours, she fully understood that there were many differences between the cultures, most of which she realized she probably wasn't aware of yet.

I will have to tread carefully and not be too bossy, listen more, instead of handing out orders so quickly. I must be respectful of their way of doing things while at the same time placing myself as a superior. This is going to be tricky. She was brought back to reality by the rain and her growling tummy.

Dropping off her goods, she went out again to find a place to eat. Popping into a café, she ordered soup and a sandwich and brought out her list.

I still didn't find a heater, she stated matter-of-factly to herself. She finished her meal and decided since it was Saturday night she was going out. She crossed the street to a pub. Stepping inside, she felt like she walked into a time warp. It was old, warm, and busy. Not the big drinker, she wasn't sure what to order. "A Diet Coke please."

"Ice?" asked the bartender.

"What?"

"Ice. Do you want ice?"

"Oh, yes, yes, sorry. I," she stuttered in her embarrassment of not understanding what the woman had asked, "I," she started again with an explanation but was interrupted by the lady,

"You from America?"

"Yes, I am. I just got here yesterday and I am still getting used to the lovely accent," she explained awkwardly.

The lady laughed and wished her luck. Charlie took a seat and looked around. Mostly everyone was drinking beer and with that thought she realized that almost everyone was male.

People were looking at her. Wishing she had brought something to read to make her appear occupied, she broke out her list, and continued watching over her paper. Glancing at her list only periodically, she took in her surroundings. People were in groups of three or four, talking easily with one another. There was music playing from the jukebox and more people shuffled in to get out of the rain. She relaxed a bit, placed her list on the table, and grabbed her pen.

For the next few hours she revised her list and tried not to dwell on how much more she needed to do.

So here she was returning to her apartment after 11 PM, wet from the rain and out of breath. She tried to get comfortable on her makeshift bed and eventually she went to sleep.

She spent Sunday morning lingering over a cup of coffee and perusing the brochures.

There is so much to do, but the first order of business today is the castle!

Armed with her tourist map, she headed out. She was happy today, determined not to obsess on what wasn't done. Walking with a spring in her step, she did the town. Old Town was everything the brochures said it would be, stunning architecture, mystery, and lore. She had a cappuccino in a pub circa 1400 and took a tour of an old townhouse set up precisely the way it was back in the days of old. Life was hard back then, she concluded. The thought made her think twice about all the complaining she had been doing. Was everything really that much harder here? Or was it just different?

The tour of the castle was unbelievable and the view out to the Firth of Forth from the Castle Esplanade was breathtaking. She learned of Princes Street Gardens, the 1:00 gun, and she was shocked to find out the castle was still used as a military base.

At the end of the Royal Mile stands Holyrood Palace, the Queen's home when she is in town. That would have to wait for another day. She made a promise to herself to come back again. She spent the rest of the day walking around taking it all in. There always seemed to be a bus or a taxi passing. She was handed leaflets for ghost tours in underground tombs and mystery walks of the haunted Closes and Wynds. The narrow walkways between the tightly squeezed buildings had been named for individuals who either lived nefarious lives near by or had met a bitter end in the location. Each seemed to have a tale and the promoters were happy to share bits and pieces to lure in tourists. She enjoyed the day even though it was cold and had rained on and off since morning.

Charlie knew she had to get back and start to prepare for tomorrow. Making her way back to her apartment, she went to her '7-11' for a bottle of red wine.

Cozied up on her temporary bed with a glass of merlot, she reviewed Mr. Moore's instructions. Convincing herself she could handle anything, she set her alarm for O dark 30 in the morning so she had time to heat the water and bathe in the sink, and then she slipped off to sleep.

CHAPTER 4

Monday

Standing before the door of her new office, Charlie took a deep breath and walked in.

"Hello, I'm Charlie Watson. I am here to see Mr. Duval," she said confidently.

"Nice to meet you, Charlie. I'm Ann. If you'll have a seat, I will call Mr. Duval."

Polite enough, perhaps this won't be so bad. After 45 minutes, Mr. Duval had still not appeared.

"Ann, did I catch Mr. Duval at a bad time? I am sure he was expecting me."

"He is on a conference call. I don't think he expected it to take this long."

After another ten minutes, a man of about 50 appeared before Charlie.

"Hello, Miss Watson, I am Doug Duval. Welcome to Edinburgh and to Johnston Banks, LTD. Why don't we go into my office?"

After being seated, Mr. Duval began to explain, "I see you met Ann. She is our receptionist and girl Friday, if you will. The office is small, only eight people. Ann will be your best source of information and she is excited about the changes. The others are quite concerned about their job security, so the feel of the office is on the tense side. I, on the other hand, have been let go."

Charlie's mouth gaped. She remembered to be careful not to flash those looks people were always telling her about. Many people close to her had warned her about the severity of her penetrating glances. Not wanting to offend, she shut her eyes for an extended blink.

"Mr. Duval, I am so sorry. No one told me. I am supposed to help with the change over - making paperwork uniform and so forth. I had no part in your dismissal."

Feeling the need to defend herself was probably not the best response, but she hated the idea that this man might think she had some doing in his demise. Panic set in. Her heart was pounding. She had taken comfort from the fact that Mr. Duval, who had been the Executive Director of the company for eleven years, would be there to assist in the changes and help quell any friction with the staff. Now that security blew out the window.

"It was nice to meet you, Charlie. Good luck." He gathered some personal affects in front of her and left.

What was probably supposed to be a very private moment for this man had most likely just turned into a very public humiliation. Now, sitting in his office, she had the terrible thought that everyone was going to suspect she had waltzed in and fired him.

Friction with the staff, forget it, mutiny is more the term now. Thanks, Mr. Moore. Thanks a lot!

What was she to do? How long could she hide in his office? What she wanted most in that brief moment was a fluffy towel, a hot shower, and her old job back. She wanted her life back as she knew it.

You cannot cry! You must not and won't! As a pep talk goes, this certainly wasn't her finest but it kept her tears of fear and frustration at bay, but for how long she didn't know. She needed a plan, and fast. By this time she figured Mr. Duval had passed Ann in the reception area and news would be spreading like wildfire. *Should she come out with guns blazing or...or what?*

I don't want to appear weak or that I can't handle this assignment. If they sense fear, they will lynch me, I'm sure.

Not knowing what she would do or say, she 'strapped on her balls' and walked to Ann.

"Well Ann, that was an unexpected twist for us all, I see." Ann was staring at her like a deer caught in headlights. And no wonder, the last person to whom she had spoken had been handed his walking papers.

"No need to fear me, Ann. I had nothing to do with this, plus which, I had no idea this was going to happen. It seems I had been set up." There were still no words from Ann. "Would you show me around the office, please, so I may meet everyone?" Ann nodded but still said nothing.

After a tour of the small office, seven handshakes, and one cup of coffee, she went back into Mr. Duval's office.

Mr. Moore had to know this was in the works. I have three more hours until he is in his office to go over this with me. Someone has to run this company and it sure as hell can't be me. Not for this salary anyway!

She went back to Ann and started her instructions as if this episode had never happened. No one talked. For almost three hours the place was in silence. And here Charlie had thought it couldn't get any worse. There was a knock on her door.

"Hi, Will, come in," she said cordially.

"Ms. Watson?"

"Please call me Charlie."

"Ms. Watson," he said again as he handed her a paper, "I am resigning."

No looks, no looks, no looks, keep that face strong and even, Lady! Think, think, think, think, think.

"Will," she said handing the paper back to him, "I won't accept it. I didn't let Mr. Duval go nor have I been instructed to release anyone. This isn't some hostile takeover like you see in the movies. Everyone here is respected for the jobs that they do and it was partly due to everyone's expertise that Johnston Banks was so

28

attractive. No one has anything to fear. Perhaps I need to address everyone regarding this matter."

A meeting was called. In her first official act, Charlie advised everyone what the game plan was, how they fit in, her role and what was expected from this day forward together. She felt everyone left feeling calmer.

"Mr. Moore, I feel I was set up. Who is going to run this company? How am I supposed to accomplish the things you sent me here to do if I am faced with no knowing leadership? These people are scared out of their minds."

She went on to tell Mr. Moore about the meeting and what had happened so far on this morning from hell. Mr. Moore was pleased with how she had handled the situation and he put his faith in her that she could carry on until someone from another office could be appointed in the next few days. His excuse for not telling her was that she had no phone. Not really an excuse, but quite accurate. *I don't think I will be asking anyone today how to go about getting a phone. Somehow, the time doesn't seem right.*

After a working lunch, she spent much of the rest of the day staring out the window at the rain. She felt a jab of self-pity.

Nothing like feeling sorry for yourself on a cold, rainy day in a foreign city and with grand confusion all around you!

Charlie put her head in her hands and took a few deep breaths hoping for some divine intervention. She truly did not know how to proceed. No one was here who could sign checks or approve applications. Not to mention the phone was ringing for Mr. Duval and Ann kept putting the calls through to her. The accents were very difficult to understand. She knew these poor people on the phone had to be going mad with her asking them to repeat themselves.

The light tap on the door snapped her back into reality.

"Ms. Watson?"

"Yes, Will?"

"I think I am still going to hand you this resignation."

"Why?" she asked sternly, with almost a hint of 'you stupid fool' in her voice.

"I work on commission, and since no one is able to tell us when a new Executive Director will be appointed, I can't trust that I will get paid on my accounts."

FUCK!

"Does everyone feel this way, Will?" she asked calmly.

"Me and Roger."

"Does Roger want to resign as well?"

"Well, he has three small children, so he has to stay. I on the other hand…" he started.

"Bring me what needs to be authorized, and I will review them and, seeing that they are accurate, I will authorize them."

Charlie didn't say it; she demanded it. Will left and returned with his accounts. After careful review, a few phone calls, and a tremendous amount of help from Ann, she signed them for payout. Thank God for Ann. Feeling quite proud of herself and thankful that she was being proactive in saving her own ass, she called Will into her office.

"Here ya go, as promised," she stated, handing him his folders back. "It is not my wish for everyone to stop producing," she continued, "it is my wish, as well as the others who came to the agreement on this merger, that production will grow due to more pulling power and higher visibility. This is a good thing, Will, not a bad one."

30

"Thank you, Ms. Watson."

Five minutes later she saw Will pass her office with his coat on and a box in his hand.

I thought it was a good speech, she reminded herself. *Woulda worked on me.*

Five o'clock wasn't going to come soon enough for Charlie. Then at 5 o'clock, Ann quit.

With her coat on, the keys in hand that Ann had given her to lock up, several bags of papers to go over, and a splitting headache, Charlie left the office after her first day. This disaster of a day was topped off with a rainy walk home.

This is definitely God punishing me for premarital sex, gotta be, what else could it be?

With no other hope left in her, she started making deals with God and confessing all her sins, while fighting the wind and rain. She felt hot tears rolling down her cheeks. She didn't want to cry, but she couldn't help it. The tears came. There was no pep talk this time. There was no strength left for one.

The sidewalks were crowded with people rushing home. The weather was fitting for her gloomy mood. With each wet step, she replayed over and over again how badly the day had gone. And with all the bags she was trying to carry, she couldn't even wipe the tears and rain from her face. Rounding the corner between two buildings, a gust of wind caught her and sent her papers flying. Dropping everything, Charlie ran after what she could, crying convulsively, while the rain dripped off her face. *WHY? WHY?* She turned back to the goods she had dropped, to see them soaking-wet in a puddle. More papers had come loose and were scattered about.

Crouching over, picking up and salvaging what she could, she heard a voice come near to her.

"Here, let me help you."

"There is no help for me," she started screaming, "The only thing that could help me is a friggin plane ticket! Thank you, thank you. I've got it, really, I don't need any help!"

Charlie stormed toward her door that was only a few feet away, fumbling for her key as she went. All hell broke loose again as papers and bags and her briefcase fell on the ground, soaking wet.

"I think you do need help," the baritone voice said coolly, as he bent near to her and grabbed up what he could.

She leaned her head the two inches to his shoulder and began to cry inconsolably in the rain.

"I'm sorry, I'm so sorry, what day is it? I can normally handle crap like this. I am so sorry." And she continued to cry and babble about heat and beds and showers, and bank accounts.

"May I help you up with these soggy things?"

Never looking at her helper or really caring what went on, Charlie nodded and up the stairs she went looking like a drowned rat in a power suit. Opening the door to her apartment, she unloaded her things and turned to her Good Samaritan for the rest, and then looked down at the floor in embarrassment. Tears still streaming down her face and out of breath, she hiccupped out, "I am really sorry, Sir. I think I have lost my mind. Thank you for your help, I truly have lost it."

He started to laugh. Charlie looked up sharply, not seeing any humor in her situation nor her embarrassment.

"Whoa, with a grimace like that, I would hate to see you when you're really mad!"

"I don't see what's so funny!" she managed to say, crying harder.

"Where's your kettle?" he said slowly, "I will put the kettle on and make you a cup of tea."

"A cup of tea?" Charlie said in disbelief at what she was hearing.

"Relax, Missy."

"Charlie," She roared, "My name is Charlie and no it's not short for anything, I assure you, its just Charlie!"

He stood there looking at her. And she looked back at him. Here was this nice man lending a helping hand and she had just about cut off his head. Not well done of her at all.

"Yet again I find myself apologizing to you. In the past five minutes, all I have managed to do is yell, cry and insult you. Please accept my apology; I am not normally on the verge of cutting a vein, I promise." Lowering her head, she waited for him to speak.

"My name is Liam. Liam Marshall. It's nice to meet you, Charlie. I take it things aren't going so hot for you today?"

"Nice to meet you Liam. No, no they are not going so well. I have certainly had better days, weeks and even years. I am sorry to have taken up so much of your time as well. I am sure you have better things to do."

"No, not really. I was off to the train to go see my mother when she called to say she wasn't feeling well and wished to reschedule. So I thought I would enjoy the lovely Scottish weather with a walk home from the train station," he said facetiously.

She managed a laugh and a smile, "Lovely Scottish weather, eh? Excellent."

"A smile. I knew I could do it," he announced, all pleased with himself.

"I don't have a teapot," she said pitifully, "I don't have much of anything, matter of fact, as I am sure you can see. Which added to my mental breakdown you just witnessed," she said pursing her lips in a 'what can I do?' sort of face.

She started again, "In America, I wouldn't let strange men in my apartment. I am at a loss on how to behave -scared? leery?"

He looked at her strangely, realizing she was probably asking him to leave but not feeling like she had the right since he helped her. "Flat."

"What's that?" Charlie said, puzzled.

"It's a flat, not an apartment. We call them flats here"

"Oh, OK," she said, confused not knowing what this had to do at all with what they were talking about.

"How about this, here is my cell phone number. Call someone and give them my name and number. Then that way you can relax and I can help you for a moment with this list you were screaming about downstairs. And you can offer me a cup of something hot, say coffee?"

"I don't know anyone here," she sulked, "I will have to call my dad in the States. And I don't have a phone"

He handed her his cell phone and she dialed her father in Maryland. This was the first time she had spoken to him since she had arrived.

"Dad, listen. I am fine and I promise to call you tomorrow but I have a gentleman here helping me. I wanted to give you his name and number since I am alone."

After a few more minutes she ended the call with an 'I love you'. Upon handing the phone back to Liam, he could see her begin to relax.

"Coffee?" he reminded her.

"I only have instant, will that be OK? And I don't have any milk because I didn't know I had a fridge until after I went grocery shopping."

She saw him glance toward her fridge. "I thought it was a dishwasher." She felt her face flush.

Putting water in the microwave, she made him a cup of coffee.

"None for you?" he asked.

"I only have one mug. Please, don't look at me like that, you wouldn't begin to understand what I have been up against."

She grabbed her merlot bottle, clinked his mug and with the classiest of smiles took a swig from the bottle.

So, for the next thirty minutes, Charlie explained everything - the shower, the hot water, the heater, the phone, the bank account, and the bed. It all came gushing out. They were sitting on the floor when she glanced up and finally noticed this man. He was in his 40's she presumed. Salt and pepper hair, cut short, dressed in jeans with a well-pressed white shirt, handsome. His eyes were an odd gray color and it was obvious he took care of himself. His 6-foot-plus frame held broad shoulders and he certainly didn't have any signs of a beer belly. She looked down quickly as he caught her looking at him.

"I've done so much belly aching, I feel embarrassed."

"Everyone needs a helping hand once in a while, especially when you're dropped off in a foreign country with no instructions. Don't worry yourself," he said encouragingly, "Let's have a look at this shower, shall we?"

One wet lady and a Good Samaritan entered the small bathroom.

"See this," he said pulling down on a cord hanging in the corner by the sink, "You have to pull that before you start your shower and when you are done, pull it again."

"Are you serious? You have to pull a cord? Never would I have known that in a million years," Charlie said disbelievingly. The shower was running, there it was, glorious water flowing from the head.

A big smile came over her face and Liam smiled just as big, knowing she was pleased. Moving on to the hot water issue, he looked around and ended up in the kitchen, where an unmarked switch was on the wall by the sink. He flicked the switch and an orange light came on above it.

"This is your hot water heater. It will probably take about twenty minutes to heat up and then you have to turn it off. Don't leave it on, it's quite dear to use. You don't have to do this for a shower; you have an electric shower. There is no central heating. You will have to purchase an electric heater."

"Quite dear?"

"That means it's expensive."

"You have no idea how much you have helped." The relief was obvious in her voice.

"Get changed. We are going to ASDA. Hurry, they close at 10, and it's already 6:30."

"Ok," she yelled over her shoulder as she headed for her bedroom, "What's ASDA?"

"Walmart, as you requested. Do you have an umbrella?"

After putting on jeans and a sweater, they walked in the cold drizzle to his house in a place he called Morningside. Charlie hadn't walked up this way yet so it was all new to her and she wished it wasn't already dark. *How many churches can there be?* They entered a neighborhood with beautiful single-family homes.

"Liam?" she questioned, "Are you married, because I don't want anyone's wife stalking me because I needed a set of sheets and a few towels?"

"No, I'm not married. So relax, there will be no stalking. I'm going inside to get the keys to the car, you are more than welcome to come in but if you are uncomfortable you may wait."

36

Was he mocking me? She chose to wait outside, with a smug look.

"Do you want to call your dad with my number plate?" he said slyly, knowing he caught her out on her safety game.

"I don't think that's necessary, he already has your details and could place you as the last person he knew I was with."

"Are all Americans paranoid?" he asked.

"I don't know. The news helps create ways for Americans to need medication; you can't help but be scared and leery part of the time."

"Did you want to drive?" he asked.

"NO, I can't drive here, I can hardly cross the street, are you kidding!" she said jokingly.

"Well, you went to the driver's side, I thought perhaps," he trailed off as she started to come to the other side of the Mercedes.

"You like making fun of me, don't you?" she flirted.

He didn't answer.

In ASDA, they each got a cart. Correction, she got a cart but he got a trolly. They went aisle by aisle, laughing, joking and shopping. They weren't halfway through the store when both cart and trolly were full.

"I am glad you have a big car, Liam. Thanks again for doing this for me, I never would have been able to carry all of this back on a bus or taxi. I do appreciate your kindness."

He gave her a smile, a sweet smile she thought. They left their two 'carts' at customer service and grabbed two more. Heaters and sheets, towels, pots, pans, plates, everything on the list! She even bought a few pictures to hang. The store was closing in 15 minutes and they had to check out. Not wanting to know the total, she handed over her company credit card while he brought the car around. The rain had returned so they loaded the packages quickly. Charlie and Liam sat for a moment in silence in the car but that silence was broken by Charlie's growling stomach.

Embarrassed, Charlie said, "I don't know if you have eaten, but it would be my pleasure to buy you dinner, if there is any place open. It would be the least I could do for all your help and company this evening."

Liam said there was a place by her flat but there might not be any place to park his car. They agreed to unload her packages and see what they could find.

The quick trip home included small talk about the past few days Charlie had been in Edinburgh, and Liam's enormous house. He lucked into a parking space. Unloading all the packages was a workout, with several trips up and down the stairs.

"I am ready for some dinner? How about you?" Charlie asked.

They went into a diner type place a few doors down and sat across from each other in the booth. After ordering, Charlie started with her questions.

"So, Liam, what do you do for a living?"

"I am a lawyer, as you Americans call them. I want you to keep my cell phone number and if you have any problems call me. I can't take you tomorrow but Wednesday we can go to a few furniture places like Ikea. Their furniture is not bulky and with a small place, that's important."

"Thank you. That would be great. Are you always this kind to strangers?"

"No, but I always had a soft spot for abused animals", he said jokingly.

"I have been called a dog many times before but I have to say that was the most polite."

The pleasant banter went back and forth for a while and the conversation was easy - her first friend in Edinburgh. They chatted about his work and hers, about where she lived in America, her family and his, and what had happened at work today.

"Well, it sounds like they got the right woman for the job. They must truly trust you to handle such a tremendous task," he said admirably.

"Thank you, but to be able to handle that today and not handle a shower leaves me wondering about my true capabilities," Charlie chuckled, shaking her head.

"These are old buildings and modern conveniences were installed, not built within, so we had to make due." The time was getting on and it was time to leave. Charlie asked for the check as she pulled out her wallet.

"Liam? What's the deal with the money here?" She asked.

"What do you mean?"

"Well, some of my bills say Bank of Scotland and the other's say Clydesdale Bank. Can anyone print money? It's so odd too how they are all different colors and sizes. The £20 note is huge! But I have yet to get a £1 note. All I keep getting are the pound coins. Is there a £1 note?"

Liam was amused by her questions. The issue with Scotland's money has been a long debated trouble spot in her history. Taking out his own wallet while motioning to Charlie to put her money away, he tried to explain, "Scotland is unique in having three banks that hold the distinct honor of being able to issue bank notes. The other bank is the Royal Bank of Scotland. Technically, Scottish notes are not legal tender. They are more of a promissory note backed by their specific bank. Most people ask 'backed by what then?' since you would normally pay an IOU with money. So it's quite technical. England and Wales can legally refuse to accept the notes even though we are all in the same country. We don't run into that so much these days however, but they certainly let you know they aren't happy about taking them."

"I have never heard of such a thing!"

"The one pound note is another story. Only the Royal Bank of Scotland is still printing them. It's quite rare to see one. And, as you pointed out, the £20 is big while conversely the £1 note is quite small. The common view on the size and color differences is that it assists the visually impaired. However, most joke it helps them when they are drunk in the dimly lit taxi's."

They both laughed together as the waitress handed Liam the check. After much protest from Charlie, Liam won paying the bill.

After thanking Liam over and over, they went their separate ways, once confirming Wednesday's date to go to Ikea.

When she walked into her apartment, she realized she hadn't left a lot of time to go through her new things. She figured she should wash her sheets and towels but realized she hadn't seen a washer and dryer in her apartment. Another hurdle. Nothing was going to be easy, nothing.

She read the directions briefly on the heaters and set up a more suitable sleeping area.

Tomorrow, she thought, *What about tomorrow?*

CHAPTER 5

Tuesday

There was no Ann, no Will and no new Executive Director. Plus she had to call her dad today. The morning meeting was something she didn't realize she was going to have. She discussed with the few left what was going to be done today. Each person had his task. She felt with each person being responsible for something daily, everyone would feel important, like a cog in a wheel. She went to her office. Her list of duties was long. She had to find someone to replace Ann. The phone was ringing and production couldn't cease. She called the Job Bank to ask for applications for Ann's job and placed an ad in the local paper. People were in and out with questions and authorizations. She was working. She was being utilized by the staff and they seemed not to mind. Things were working. Good.

Sipping her coffee, she decided to clear up the desk and make it more appropriate for herself since she seemed to have inherited the office and no one was there to tell her she couldn't.

Why not? Why can't I have the big office with the leather chair and the window!

Looking through files and organizing paper clips, returning messages and getting the IT department to change over emails, things were progressing slowly, but progressing. The new paperwork had been ordered and should be delivered in five days. There was end-of-the-month paperwork that would need to be completed and new quotas determined for each representative. There was a lot to do. She continued rifling through Mr. Duval's things to get some sort of organization. She placed his personal things in a box thinking someone must know how to get hold of him.

Charlie decided to get out of the office and grab a bite to eat. Sitting in a small Italian restaurant, she gave herself a pep talk about her capabilities and why she had been chosen to come to Scotland. *I can do this.*

"Well hello, fella!," petting the head of the little dog that had wandered over.

"I am so sorry," a voice came, grabbing up the pooch. "He normally stays right with me."

"No problem. He is a cutie. What's his name?"

"Taco." A perfect name for a mini Chihuahua.

"That's excellent. My name is Charlie."

"Hi. I am Adele. Nice to meet you."

"Nice to meet you too."

"Are you here by yourself?" Adele asked.

"Yes. Just a quick lunch."

"I am alone as well; do you care to join me?

"That would be great, sure."

The two girls chatted, getting to know each other. Adele lived a few blocks away from Charlie's apartment and invited her to the quiz at the local pub next Monday.

"What's a quiz?" Charlie asked.

"It's fun! I go with a bunch of my girlfriends. You can be on our team. Each week the Quizmaster prepares questions that he reads aloud to everyone to answer on their answer sheets. There is a round on music, movies, current affairs, history, and then general trivia. When the quiz is finished you pass in your sheets and he checks them. The team that comes in first place gets a round of free drinks. Mostly everyone sits around drinking and having a good time, laughing at all the nostalgia the quizmaster can dig up with his silly questions. We don't win very often, but the pub has a good group of people."

Charlie decided it would be great to go and they exchanged phone numbers.

I have another friend.

Later that afternoon, Charlie called her father as promised and filled him in on all the details. He felt bad for his daughter but praised and encouraged her. She felt homesick when she got off the phone. She decided to call Liam to thank him again and to give him her office number in case he needed it.

"Liam?"

"Yes?"

"Hi, it's Charlie."

"Hello there, how are things going for you today?"

"Not bad actually, thanks. I was calling to give you my office number in case you need to change plans for tomorrow."

Liam noted the number but assured her things would be fine for tomorrow; he also wanted to pick up a few things. They set a time of 6 PM, which didn't give her much time after work. She told him about her new friend and the quiz. After a few jokes about hot water and wine bottles, they said goodbye. Charlie felt excited about tomorrow night.

This Liam was a nice guy. She hadn't had much luck finding them lately. After a few failed relationships, Charlie had been content to leave that area of her life alone and focus on her career. Most of the men in her past had seemed to be filled with fluff. They weren't driven to achieve nor did they seem to be eager to explore, whether it be a museum in Washington DC or a wine festival. They tended to be happy at a local bar or with a sports channel. There was no culture, no excitement.

How many guys, when you date, do all the same stuff – go out to dinner, movies, the beach, same old crap and the dreaded redneck softball game – aaaahhh.

How many softball games can a woman really watch and still act supportive of his team?

No one ever says why don't we go to the National Cathedral for church on Sunday followed by a brunch at the Smithsonian, or a play. Everything is the same boring stuff - no creativity. I mean they are in their 30's for godsake – Can we get some adult culture?

She chalked it up to looking in the wrong places. But now this Liam - he seemed to be different.

CHAPTER 6

The desk is big. Some of the letters are wearing off the keyboard. Mr. Duval must have worked hard. I wonder why they let him go. I wonder how he told his wife. Why would they fire him?

Charlie was startled from her thoughts by a stern knock on the door and then an entrance by Mr. Duval.

"Well, hello, Mr. Duval! I didn't expect to see you. Is everything ok? How are you?" Charlie inquired, hoping maybe he would give a positive answer like 'They gave me my job back.'

"I seemed to have left a few things behind in my haste and confusion. Do you mind?"

"Uhm – well" she hesitated. In her conscience she knew she should not allow him. He could do many destructive things, especially since he seemed quite bothered and irritated.

Charlie squeaked out, "Actually, the computers have all been cleared out and redone with new software. I put your few personal items over there." She motioned to the box in the corner. "There is nothing more for you." Not stating this with much conviction whatsoever, she prayed hard he would buy it.

"I was after a few personal files I had left," he said, walking to the desk with purpose. Feeling the pressure, Charlie knew she had one last attempt, "I am sorry, Mr. Duval. I have disposed of everything and created my own files. There is nothing here that is yours from before." Standing as she finished, she hoped it appeared powerful.

"If I could have a quick look, I am sure...."

"Nothing's here!" Charlie said, cutting him off. "Please leave." *Please leave, please leave,* she prayed.

He was visibly angry. His face was red and sweat had started to bead above his lip. Without a word he turned and left. Breathing a sigh of relief, Charlie was caught completely off guard when he re-entered, walked directly to the desk, pushed her out of the way and shoved her to the floor. He then opened the desk drawer and removed a half dozen flash drives.

"Mr. Duval, that is no longer your property. You cannot take those! They belong to the company," she yelled.

"They belong to me!" he raged as he left.

Is there security in this building?
"Roger?" Charlie called out. Charlie called Roger's phone. No answer. Shaking, she left her office to get him and realized the place was empty. There were only minutes until 5:00 PM. Charlie was on edge. Each breath echoed in her ears. She walked slowly through the office feeling as though Mr. Duval was going to jump out and attack her around every corner. She double-checked to make sure the place was really empty before she left, locking the door behind her.

Leaving the office, she was wondering if she should call Mr. Moore and tell him. *I'll think on it*, she decided. *Boy, I bet Duval is going to be pissed when he realizes one of those drives is missing.*

Hitting the street, Charlie felt odd. She wrapped her coat tighter but the feeling didn't go away. *What's wrong?* She should have called Mr. Moore. *Something's wrong. Not something... All of it.*

Charlie learned years ago to trust her intuition. She couldn't always place the 'who, what, where, when and how,' but she knew when things weren't right. Something wasn't right and she wasn't convinced it was just Mr. Duval's show a moment ago. She turned to head back to the office. She would call Mr. Moore to ask his take on the issue. Charlie was breathing heavier; a sick

46

impending feeling of doom came over her. She turned back again and then one more time. She was caught. She didn't feel good about either going back to the office or heading home. Her steps were heavy with dread filling her stride. Each option of where to go and what to do seemed tainted. *Which way Charlie? Where do you go?*

She ducked into a small market to collect her thoughts. All she could think of was to call Liam for help. She looked out the window and spotted two phone booths. What was she to say to Liam? "I feel like something's wrong" - not an ingenious statement.

"Liam – I am so glad you answered. It's Charlie. Something's wrong." She choked out.

"What do you mean?" he asked with deep concern.

"I really don't know, but something's wrong." Charlie proceeded to tell him about Mr. Duval, how no one was in the office, how he shoved her and then the walk home with her foreboding gut feeling. He half laughed and told her to calm down. 'Calm Down' was the one statement that drove her nuts. She gritted her teeth to keep from saying something she would regret. She rolled her eyes as well at what she really expected his reaction to be. Like some super hero? She had only known the guy a few days. She thought of all he had done to help. Embarrassed and beaten, she whispered into the phone, "But something's wrong."

"Ok. Where are you?" he conceded.

He was coming to get her. She didn't feel relieved; she felt protected. This led her to believe that perhaps she was in danger. It felt more of an answer than any other for her feelings so far.

The wait for Liam was a nervous one. Charlie's eyes darted in every direction, watching for anything that seemed out of place. She studied everyone's face and expression, looking for answers to questions she wasn't sure she even knew. Everyone was a suspect in a make believe plot. Paranoia might be the worst feeling in the world. Fear is a debilitating emotion generating actions that reach from unreasonable to insane.

Each second that passed was turning Charlie's mind into a dangerous tornado on a reckless path, concocting twisted schemes to explain Mr. Duval's behavior. A light dew appeared across her forehead as the rush of her panic set in. Her mind was running away with her.

When Liam arrived, she ran to the car as if she were protecting herself from enemy gunfire. She sank into the front seat and looked over at him and his thoughts read clearly – Now what?!

Sounding worried and confused, she confessed, "I don't know what to say, Liam. Something's wrong."

With all of the emotions running through her - embarrassment, confusion, fear- she was paralyzed at the sudden, overwhelming feeling to crawl on his lap, snuggle in and start kissing him all over- his lips, face, neck and to smell him, touch him.

Oh my God Charlie! She clinched her eyes tight and shook her head to clear her thoughts. She reached for the door handle, jumped out of the car and began walking – fast.

Charlie Watson, you've gone off the edge, she scolded herself.

"Charlie!" Liam yelled, "Charlie"

She stopped and slowly turned around, head lowered. Standing directly in front of her for what seemed like forever, he grabbed her shoulders and tilted her to him. His arms went around her and she nestled into his chest. After a brief moment Charlie muttered, "I'm not a wimp." But she still didn't let go of him or make one move.

"Who said you were a wimp?" he asked consolingly.

"That must be what you are thinking. Honestly, Liam – I am a capable woman. Something's going on

48

and I feel like a pawn. I don't know what it is but I'm going to find out. You may think I am a fruit loop but you wait and see. I'll be right!!"

Standing firm, staring right into his face with certainty oozing from every pore in her body, her mouth gaped open as she realized how handsome and attractive he truly was, she softened, melted actually, transfixed on his eyes. *Look away,* she said to herself or so she thought.

"What?" he questioned.

"I'm not a wimp," she whispered again.

Liam grabbed her hand and walked her back to the car. Opening the door, he put her in. Her briefcase was still there. *He must think I am a nutcase.*

"Come on, Loopy. We'll go to your place, grab you some clothes and you'll stay at my house tonight. Right or wrong, something's got you spooked."

Yeah, I'm spooked all right. Is it work or is it you?

In a split second Charlie's focus changed. *I'm spending the night! Ally's gonna love this one.* Now she had other things to worry about.

CHAPTER 7

Walking inside his house, she couldn't get over the size compared to her place. It was more of an American house. It was very clean and perfectly decorated, masculine, yet warm and classic.

"Wow," *another brilliant statement from the mouth of Charlie Watson.*

"I'll say thank you to that, I think," Liam teased. "I see you are short on vocabulary today," winking at her.

"Drink?" he asked holding up a bottle of wine.

"Why not! Half a glass. I'm not a big drinker."

He handed her a beautiful crystal glass that she admired for a moment. Charlie took a long sip.

"I'll go build the fire. Why don't you get changed," he suggested.

"Changed into what?" Charlie said horrified. "All I brought were pajamas that consist of sweat pants and a tee shirt. It's not really what I consider fashion fit for company."

"Well, that's what I am going to put on and we'll make dinner and lounge in front of the fire. Sound good?"

"Where do I get changed?"

Liam took Charlie upstairs. She saw his office - a big cherry desk, lots of papers, and she believed she smelled cigars. He opened the door right off his office. The light revealed a bright room with yellows and blues, a big queen size bed and a bathroom.

"This is so nice, Liam," she said turning toward him with a smile. "Thank you again for all your help. I hope one day you'll thank me for something."

She felt bad, like she was taking advantage of his kindness. Perhaps he had made other plans for tonight.

"Liam? I hope I have not intruded on any of your plans..."

"No, Loopy," he cut her off, shaking his head, "I had nothing on for this night. I was going to make dinner and sit in front of the fire and that's what I'm still going to do but as a bonus, I now have company."

"Are you sure?"

"YES, Charlie, I am sure."

She changed and had the dilemma - bra or no bra? At home it would have been no bra, but she couldn't bring herself to that here. She had to keep it on – *argh*. *Yeah, I better,* she convinced herself. The fire was already crackling by the time she came down. He had changed as well.

"Come on, Loops, let's eat!" They were in the fridge pulling stuff out and chatting about what to have.

"Hey?" Charlie said all excited, "do you have chicken bouillon?"

"Yes."

"OK then, go read the paper or whatever it is that you do. I have dinner covered."

With a questionable smirk, he did; he went to read the paper. It had been a long time since there had been a woman in his house and even longer since one had made him dinner. He wasn't sure what to make of it.

In the kitchen, Charlie was writing odes in her head to her mother, who had taught her a quick, simple yet utterly fit-for-a-king chicken-and-wine-sauce recipe. She was stomping around looking for everything and she was not only amazed that he had everything but that it was all exactly where she would keep it. Rice was boiling, chicken was frying, and veggies were steaming.

"Where will we be dining?" Charlie yelled through to the other room.

"How about in there?" he answered.

"Great!"

Liam came in to check on her and it smelled delightful. And she really wasn't making a mess, he noted. He refilled their wine glasses and sat at the table, watching this creature who was completely at home in his kitchen.

She was oblivious, he thought, that he was even there. She talked to herself a few times, tasted her creation in progress, and searched his cabinets for whatever it was she apparently needed. For a whole five minutes, he was captivated by her. She wasn't a beauty queen or Hollywood material but he was riveted. He wondered why. She seemed to be quite adaptable, he thought. Rolling with whatever comes her way. She was enjoying herself and he enjoyed watching. Charlie took out some plates and turned to set the table.

"OOH!" she jumped, "I didn't know you were here." She handed him the dishes, silverware and napkins and he made up the table.

Charlie had made a stupendous meal. She knew he loved it. He kept saying it, so that helped. However, in her household a good meal was judged by how many people went for second helpings. Charlie didn't relax until Liam refilled his plate.

Conversation was easy and the wine bottle was empty. Cracking open the second bottle, they sat at the table and relaxed. No one had any intentions of moving – just enjoying. Charlie felt good. She felt she had repaid him partly for all his help. She made a mental note to bring him dinner again in a few days. Laughing and carrying on like old friends, Charlie stood to clear the table. She grabbed several things off the table and started walking over to the sink.

"NO, No. Fair is fair," he shouted, "you cooked, so I do the dishes."

"Are you crazy?" she replied, "for all you have done for me the least I can do is a few dishes."

After going back and forth a few times, they decided to do the dishes together. *Everything is easy with Liam*, she thought. *He is so not complicated.*

Charlie realized they were somewhat flirting with each other – neither one making any real big jousts but there was a playfulness between them. She told herself to lay off the wine and, as if he was reading her mind, he handed her a full wine glass. She felt that her cheeks were already flushed. *What the hell,* she thought, *Let loose, relax,* she encouraged herself. *You've had a bad day.*

The dishwashing chore turned to snapping towels at ankles and splashing each other. *Such childish play for adults*, Charlie noted. In the midst of this fun, the doorbell rang. They looked at each other with surprise, feeling like they'd gotten caught. Charlie immediately started straightening her appearance. Charlie was, however, standing right in front of the side door, which happened to be half glass. Liam leaned a few inches to the left, peering over her shoulder. Charlie instinctively did the same.

Charlie's eyes must have bulged as they met the most beautiful woman she had ever seen. The woman had gorgeous, shiny chestnut hair. Her makeup was perfect and she was dressed to the nines in a smart business suit of gray pinstripes. The woman took a look at Charlie and Charlie felt the woman's eyes look her up and down quickly.

Liam moved to open the door, collecting himself. Charlie was sure she saw his jaw tighten and he looked ashen.

"Hello, Rebekah," he stated calmly.

"Hello, Liam," she said, almost as a question. Charlie wanted to die. She didn't know who this woman was but she was sure that she didn't like her one bit.

"I was away on business when I received your message, perhaps I should have called first," she stated, looking down her nose at Charlie.

"Charlie, this is Rebekah. Bek this is Charlie." Liam's eyes were on the floor.

"Nice to meet you," Charlie said, hoping her voice wasn't betraying her. Rebekah half smiled and grunted royally, while stepping inside.

"I'll get your things for you," Liam said while walking to a box in the corner of the room.

Another box in a corner, Charlie thought. Glancing quickly at the contents, she could see it was personal stuff. Charlie got a chill as the tape of today's earlier event with Mr. Duval played in her mind. Boxes and big desks. When Liam handed her the box, Rebekah turned to leave.

"Well, I will leave you to it. Thanks."

Liam closed the door. Charlie was staring at him. She felt like a trespasser at that moment. She was on someone else's property. Seconds passed when Liam cleared his throat, "She uh... well, ...you see, she...her things," he couldn't get it together.

Charlie was sorry for his discomfort but she did want to hear, she wanted to know ...desperately. She was deflated, kicked in the stomach. She didn't know why she felt like this but she did. She turned to continue the last bit of the dishes. She said nothing. After all, he owed her no explanation. She was only staying here because he was being kind. She didn't feel good; it didn't feel good. Going home didn't feel good, going back to work didn't feel good, and now, being here didn't feel good. What a mess it all was.

*****

Wiping her hands dry on the towel, Charlie was still trapped in silence as Liam continued to stand there speechless.

"It's no big deal, Liam," she said convincing herself she was right. "I hope this isn't going to spoil the fun night we were having. We still have a half bottle of wine and a fire burning." After that came out of her mouth she cringed in her embarrassment. *That sounded bad. Everything was bad. That sounded like sex and.... Oh... God I want to die. How could I have said that?*

"Well, that didn't sound right," she chuckled, trying to make light of her awkward statement. Liam still had not moved nor said a word. *What was going through his mind?* He looked tortured. He looked like he was in pain. Drawing her own conclusion about who and what that was, she moved. Charlie grabbed his hand and walked him into the living room. She parked him on the couch where his paper was waiting and then handed him his wine. She settled in front of the fire and sipped the rest of her wine while perusing a section of the newspaper. All in all it was the longest two minutes of her life. He was obviously hurt by this woman. She had probably devoured his sweet soul as an appetizer.

I wonder how long they have been broken up. I wonder how long they went out. Should I speak or wait till he is ready? Without thinking she climbed on the couch and rested her head on his lap, grabbed his arm around her and started lightly caressing it. She closed her eyes. She felt his other hand start playing with her hair.

"I am sorry," he stated matter of factly.

"For what?" Charlie said evenly.

"For not handling that as well as I should have," he sounded angry now.

"How were you supposed to handle it?"

"I don't know, truthfully." Liam was shaking his head slightly, she guessed at himself.

"Everyone has an ex, Liam, some are just more painful than others. Like I said, no big deal."

"That wasn't my ex, Charlie. That was my sister."

"Oh!" she said sounding a little too excited. *This changes everything.*

"Well, what's wrong with her coming by? Or shouldn't I ask?"

"Two years ago she ran off with my fiancée. I caught them in bed together. I have not seen either of them since."

"Really?!" You couldn't miss the astonishment in her voice. Yet another mind boggling statement.

"Really" was all he said back. Charlie figured she would leave it at that. *A fiancée. A lesbian. Betrayal on both sides. Wow!*

Liam continued to play with her hair. It felt nice and she wasn't about to complain. Perhaps she shouldn't have come up on the couch but it was too late now. She had a million questions but they would have to wait.

"I am glad I was here so you didn't have to be here alone when she came by."

"Me too," was his simple reply. *Good enough,* she thought.

The room was warm and she was full from dinner. She hoped she wouldn't fall asleep. It had been a long time since she was snuggled into a man. But after the thoughts that ran through her mind earlier this evening, she was concerned for herself. It would be nice to run her fingers down the strong chest of a man. To sleep next to a warm body and wake up next to one too. To not have to make so many decisions alone. She was sounding like a desperate lonely woman when in reality she was perfectly fine on her own, perhaps a bit horny at times, but otherwise ok. It was only 8:30 PM.

56

*****

Charlie's mind turned to work. *Mr. Duval knew exactly what he wanted and he knew exactly where it was. I wonder what was on those flash drives. Why did he want them back? I should tell Mr. Moore because he could have all sorts of confidential information on them that he is taking to a competitor to steal clients. What if people had still been in the office? Would he still have come in and shoved me?*

"Liam?"

"Yes?"

"Can I call my boss in America?"

"Of course."

He started to get up, but hesitated one last second to squeeze her hand. She started up after him.

"No, no, I will bring it to you, relax."

She lay there on the couch like she lived in the house. She quickly sat up. She didn't want him to think she was moving in. *Women - always thinking ahead.*

He handed her the phone and she dialed. He sat back down on the couch and pulled her back to him. It seemed natural. Charlie spoke with her boss for a half hour telling him all she had experienced. He didn't know what to make of it either. She didn't tell him she had one of the flash drives. No one needed to know that. It wasn't important. She asked why Duval was let go and Mr. Moore gave her some answer about resistance to the new regime and lying about accounts that were secured. The reasons seemed legit to her.

After hanging up, they stayed on the couch until it was time to retire.

"I'll see you in the morning, what time do you have to get up?" he asked.

"6:30 AM. Is there an alarm clock?"

"I'll wake you," he said.

He went to his room and she to hers.

Charlie watched as he closed his door. Charlie lay there and thought about the dinner and the playfulness they seemed to have. *I could get used to that,* was her last thought before she fell asleep.

Wednesday

Morning arrived for Charlie with a knock on the door and the smell of coffee. Liam sat on the bed with the mug in his hand, "Good morning, Sleeping Beauty."

Never the morning person, Charlie grunted, very unladylike.

"Whoa, I see we have a morning person here. Up and at'em, Little Lady!!" he said throwing back the covers. With that, Charlie squealed and grabbed quickly for the covers; she wasn't wearing any pants! Liam started laughing and fighting with her over the covers. She was awake now and he knew it.

"Stop, stop!!" she yelled, laughing, taking pleasure in the game.

"So I see we sleep in a tee shirt. Consider it noted. Next time I won't knock!" He was pleased with himself.

After a quick shower, she went downstairs with her empty mug. She was dying for a refill.

"I am taking you to work and I will stay with you for a while," he announced.

"Don't you have work to do today, Liam?"

"No, I am off today. No cases, no court."

They walked out the door and into the car. The ride took minutes. They parked in the garage and walked to her building. She felt as though people were looking at her or them - she wasn't sure which. She had two interviews today for Ann's position. The computer change-over finally was to take place, the one she had lied to

58

Mr. Duval about. People were going to be in and out all day.

Once in her office she sat at the desk and laughed.

"What's so funny?" Liam asked.

"I don't fit behind this desk. I inherited this office when they fired Mr. Duval. I sort of stayed," she said, chuckling as though she were a kid who got away with something.

"I think you look great there. It suits you." He was being kind, she was sure.

"I'll get some coffee," she said.

The staff was arriving and she knew she needed to do her morning address. She sat in the middle of the staff and spoke.

"The week is winding down. Let's finish strong."

With that, she had everyone share where they were on their monthly goals, what they had working, and what they thought they could close. She was writing it on the dry erase board and came back with the figures. She stated weekly and monthly what everyone had closing. It exceeded the goals she was given by Mr. Moore for the month. She felt a jolt of excitement.

"This looks good, everyone. Let me know if you need help with anything and I will do my best to give it. If we exceed what is expected of us, it will make all your stock options more valuable. There are two more weeks in the month. Stay strong and prospect. Keep that pipeline full."

Satisfied with her morning meeting, she returned to her now-empty office. *Where is he?*

"Are you sure they aren't planning to keep you in charge?" he said, appearing out of nowhere in her doorway, sounding amazed at her performance.

"No way, I am an Operations Manager slash Executive Organizer. I am not an Executive Director slash

President!! I just don't want more people to quit. It's tough enough I have to sort through work from the people who have gone and close the deals they left behind."

"So you can close deals too?"

"Well yeah, I know this game inside and out. The only reason Mr. Moore didn't move me to sales was because he would forget where his glasses were if I weren't around!" she stated proudly. Liam nodded as if he already expected such an answer.

Liam hung around and drank his coffee. The 'real' workday began. The phone was ringing, people were coming to her and she was working. He liked watching. She was capable and she wasn't a wimp. She was strong and knowledgeable. After her first interview, he was impressed.

Her questions were pointed, deliberate, and proved to have a purpose behind what answer she was looking for. She was sharp. *She would make a good lawyer,* he thought.

It was time to go and let her get on with it. Liam rose, "I see you have things under control here, so I will talk to you later. Have a good day." He gave her a quick, unexpected kiss and said goodbye over his shoulder. Charlie stood there shocked. *He just kissed me. Now how the hell am I supposed to concentrate all day?*

The afternoon went quickly, even though she was daydreaming all day. He had kissed her and she had liked it, a lot. She liked him, a lot. Admitting it to herself was a mistake. It changed the playing field, a lot. It had been a long time since she was excited over a man, maybe a little too long. She seemed to be saying that too, a lot.

After lunch, work was busy. Investors were calling and she had no idea how to field their questions. She sent emails to get the status on the start of the server conversion but she was told it would be delayed for a

60

few more days due to licensing discrepancies. The phone would not stop ringing.

"Hello. Johnston Banks."

"Charlie?" came a familiar voice.

"Hi Liam!" she answered, trying to hide her excitement that faded quickly when she thought he was going to cancel their shopping trip.

"Do you want to slip over to the bank real quick and I will help you with your bank account?"

"Thanks but they said I can't get one until I have two check stubs from here."

"Come on over, I'll sort it for you."

She let Roger know she would be gone and headed to the bank. *How is he going to pull this off?*

He looked phenomenal! He had on a navy blue suit that made him look like royalty.

"Wow, look at you!" Charlie sang.

"Mr. Marshall, is this the other party for whom you were waiting?" asked a middle aged, pudgy man.

"Yes, Mr. Bailey," he said staidly.

Charlie was introduced to the bank manager, and in minutes forms were being filled out and bank codes chosen. She was stunned at how Liam had managed to make this happen and that he even remembered. Leaving the bank, Charlie looked up at him, "You are amazing!"

"See you in a few hours," he called out to her as he walked briskly in the opposite direction."

Thank you, God, for sending me Liam. And then the thought hit her. *Who the hell is he that he can command a bank manager like that?*

The last few hours of work went on forever. She was like a kid on Christmas Eve. Rushing home, she grabbed a bite to eat and was changing when the door buzzer sounded earlier than she expected. She let him up.

"Sorry, I am not ready yet. I'll be one more minute. Make yourself at home." she called over her shoulder from the bathroom.

"Everything go ok at work today for you?" he inquired.

"Yeah, actually."

"Good. Glad to hear you won't be having a meltdown tonight."

They arrived at Ikea, which was about 20 minutes away. They grabbed their pencils for ordering.

"I made a list so I wouldn't forget anything," she stated proudly. She took the list out of her pocket and handed it to him. He looked it over.

"A loveseat?"

"Yeah. I figured that would be smaller than a sofa and it's only me so I don't want something so big it takes up too much room."

"We call then settees."

With Liam's help, she found everything on her list and a few things that weren't. Then they hit Liam's list. He picked up a few things that they were able to take home. With all their packages in his car, they set in for the journey home.

"I have an embarrassing question to ask you," Charlie spilled out.

"Oh yeah and what is that?"

"Do you know anything about laundromats?"

"Not really. Why? You don't have a washer?"

"Nope! She answered. In America, well, laundromats are associated with poor people and 'down-and-outs'.

"A lot of people use them here because their places are quite small and the water and electric are expensive. Not to mention the machines themselves. So it's no big deal here. We'll find you one. Do you want to go for a drink?" he asked. "It's only 9 o'clock."

"Sure. Why not?" Charlie agreed.

They went to her place to unload her purchases and then back to his place to drop off the car. By 10 o'clock they were seated in a cozy bar with a fireplace. People were looking at them and Charlie was uncomfortable.

"I feel like everyone is looking at us?" she questioned.

"Don't worry about them," he said brushing them off. Charlie asked about his work and after a few short answers, she figured he didn't want to talk about it. So she didn't push the subject.

She asked if his mom was feeling better, about his dad, and other family. Liam had two sisters, both younger than he. They lived out of town toward Glasgow. His father was older than his mother and didn't get out much. Liam went to see them a few times a month. His mother periodically came out to stay with him for a night when she wanted to do some shopping.

Charlie enjoyed his company. *He is very charming. He is also very good looking – possibly the reason everyone is looking at us. They are probably thinking what the hell is HE doing with HER.*

"I should probably go home," Charlie declared. "These days are draining and sleep seems to be the only thing rejuvenating me."

Liam, ever the gentleman, walked her home. "Thanks for taking me shopping... again – I may add. You've made getting settled here so much easier."

Charlie was embarrassed at everything he had done for her already in the three days she had known him.

"No problem. I've enjoyed the company," he offered.

"Did you want to come in?" she asked hesitantly.

"No, no. I know you need your sleep. I'll talk to you soon. Get a good night's sleep."

Charlie closed the door but all of a sudden she wasn't so tired. Her head was comfortably on the pillow but her mind was on Liam.

CHAPTER 8

Thursday

Work was filled with issue after issue. All Charlie seemed to be doing today was putting out fires. One by one, she tackled each problem, one after the other. The computers were acting up, the phones were ringing, and people were coming into the office. She had to keep getting up to greet the visitors.

There is no way I am going to get anything accomplished if I am continually interrupted.

Charlie was certain she couldn't keep up this pace for much longer. Hearing the door chime, she got up from her desk again.

"Liam! Hi. What are you doing here?" She practically skipped over to him. She quickly decided that she had better play it a little cooler.

"I thought I would pop in and see how you were doing."

"Well, today's been quite hectic. I'm pulling my hair out," Charlie laughed.

"I am sure you have things under control. I have invited my mother down and we are all going to dinner tonight." He saw the look on her face.

"Is something wrong? Do you not want to go?" He seemed slighted, even insulted perhaps.

"No, no that's fine. I am shocked that's all"

"Why?"

"I am not sure really, I am..." Charlie scrambled for words, "I am honored by the invite. I would love to meet your mother."

"I will call you and let you know what time dinner will be. Whatever and wherever it is, dress well, it will be fancy. Mother's not a cheap date."

"Nor am I," Charlie joked. Again he gave her a quick kiss.

"I'll see you tonight," he called out.

The rest of the day was hectic but productive. She called Mr. Moore to inquire about her pay and that of the others. There was still no progress on finding a replacement for Mr. Duval. She had also scheduled several more interviews for the beginning of next week. Liam called as promised and dinner was set for 7 PM.

I'm meeting his mother.

She headed home, eager for what the night would unfold. *I need to shave my bikini line.* It was then Charlie realized she was going to need help. A thought like that doesn't come into your brain unless there are feelings involved. Help came in the form of a 'call box' and a call to Ally.

Giving Ally the Reader's Digest version of what was going on, they sounded more like two school girls with a crush on the high school quarterback than two grown adults. It was good to talk to her and Charlie was glad for the advice. "Just 'be' yourself, Charlie. Be true to *you*. From the sound of it, a man like Liam doesn't need to play games. He only wants to go to dinner with you and his mother. Have fun and enjoy it," Ally had said.

Liam picked her up at 6:30; they were meeting his mother at the restaurant. He looked gorgeous. He wore a pair of tan chinos with a navy blue blazer. Charlie had decided on a camel pant's suit with an eggshell blouse and pearls, always classic. Liam let out a whistle as she got in the car. "My lady, your chariot awaits!" he heralded.

"Why thank you, kind sir," she said shyly.

"You look really nice, Charlie."

"Thank you, as do you."

Liam briefed her on his mother, Mrs. Charlotte Montgomery Marshall, and her meticulous demeanor. Along with her love of all things expensive, her keen fashion sense, and her unbelievable ability to make ordering even the simplest glass of water sound elegant. All it did was make Charlie nervous.

Bocelli's was an elite Italian restaurant in the heart of the city center. The stress started immediately. *I hope I know what fork to use, I hope I don't spill any thing, I hope I can order properly. I am going to screw this up royally,* she concluded.

"Mother!" Liam said with a loving formalness.

"Well, Liam, you are looking as clever as ever, and you must be Charlie," she said turning her attention.

"It's a pleasure to meet you, Ma'am." It was the best she could do. They all sat.

"I love your pearls, Charlie. Are they Cartier?"

"Actually they were a gift from my grandmother for my Confirmation. They are from Italy," Charlie stated proudly, fielding the first of many questions she felt were going to be rapid-fired at her. She had a vision of herself being in a batting cage with the balls being hurled at her head.

"Well, they are lovely," noted Mrs. Charlotte Montgomery Marshall.

"Thank you," Charlie stated, as though she heard that all the time.

"So, Liam, your case is going well?" his mother inquired.

"We are at a standstill," Liam started. With that the conversation was underway and food was ordered and eaten. As coffee and espressos were being served the conversation was directed at Charlie.

"Charlie, Liam tells me that your firm sent you. How are you finding Edinburgh so far?"

"Well thanks to your kind son, I am adapting far better than I would have alone. In America, I could handle whatever came my way but I have had a few curve balls thrown at me here that were quite unexpected. So thanks to Liam's helping hand, many disasters have been averted."

Charlie spoke of what she did, what the firm was about and how the conversion was going. By the time things were wrapping up, she wasn't as nervous as she was before. *I wonder if this was a date.*

As they said their goodbyes and Charlie got in the car with Liam, things became uncomfortable. Not something she had expected. There was an awkward silence while Liam started the short drive home. *HOME!* She thought. That was the problem. I wonder if we are going to his place or mine. Idle chit-chat was all she was capable of as he pulled up in front of her place.

"Thank you so much for the lovely dinner, and your mother is very charming. Thank you for including me in your plans tonight." Her statement was sincere and heartfelt.

"No problem, I am glad you came along. It's difficult with Mother; she can be hard work and having some one else there made the conversation better. So thank you."

"Would you like to come up for a coffee or something?"

"No, I best not, I am going to go home and work on some things and get to the office early tomorrow. But I will walk you up."

At the top of her stairs, with her key in the door, she gave him a quick hug and another thank you. Over his shoulder he whispered, "I'll call you tomorrow to make sure all is well at work."

"I promise not to need saving tomorrow, I will handle tomorrow all by myself," she said jokingly like a first grader learning to tie her shoes. He laughed and said he had faith in her.

Once inside she got changed and made a cup of tea. While sorting through her mail, she reflected on the past four days - spending the night, the dinner, and Rebekah. *So he was engaged.* She felt a pang of jealousy.

There was a lot of mail for the old tenants.

"What the hell!," Charlie yelled. Everything had gone black in the house. "Can I not get through one day without an issue?" She felt the wall and tried the switch. She had no idea where the fuse box was and of course she had no flashlight. She couldn't even remember if she had bought a candle. *I can't believe this.* Groping for her keys and her money, she put on her coat and went to the phone booth. *'She is incompetent' - that is what he is going to think. She is incapable of being alone for one second.*

"Liam? I know I said I was not going to need saving but in true Charlie style I have encountered an issue that has prevented me from keeping true on my promise for even a half hour."

She half expected him to start yelling like a father would at a teenager who had wrecked the car or brought home a bad report card. However, in true Liam style, he asked. "And what might that be?"

Trying to not sound like a whiny baby but rather a sophisticated, businesswoman, "Well, it appears I have blown a fuse and I have no idea where the fuse box is nor do I have a flashlight to look for one. Why I would blow a fuse with two lights on I have no idea but the fact remains that I have no lights, nor heat for that matter. I was wondering if by some chance you might know where I would first look for one so I may be able to function in my house for the rest of the evening, seeing it's only 9:30. Please consider in your answer the total embarrassment of my call and the fact that I am in a phone booth in my pajamas."

Amused at the thought, Liam muttered, "Honestly, I have no idea."

"OK," Charlie said dismayed, "Well thanks anyway, I'll sort it out tomorrow. Sorry to have bothered you yet again, Liam."

"No problem, Dear, have a good night." And they each hung up their phones.

"Well, that sucks!" It looked like an early night for her. Walking into her dark apartment, she went into the bedroom and crawled into her pseudo bed. *Mental note: Get candles and a flashlight. And a phone!*

She had met his mother. *I wonder why he did that. I wouldn't have done that. Why did I go? Should I have said 'no thanks'? Should I have offered to pay something?*

Replaying the events in her mind, she couldn't help but feel she had committed some etiquette *gaffe*.

What the hell is that? Sitting straight up in bed, scared out of her mind, she realized it was her buzzer for guests. *Liam,* she thought. *He came.* She walked carefully to the hall phone and answered, "Hello?"

"Let me up, Loopy."

He came in. With the light from the hallway she saw he was in his pj's too.

"Liam, you didn't have to come over here. I will be fine until tomorrow morning."

He had a flashlight and a candle.

"Be careful." she said. "There is a mug of tea somewhere on the floor in the living room."

He searched everywhere. He found nothing. Back in the hallway, still with the door open for light, they discussed what to do.

"I have not paid a bill yet," Charlie said. "Matter of fact, I have not notified any companies I am here. I probably am not going to have gas for my stove here pretty soon, now that I think about it. I never thought about this kind of stuff until now."

He just looked at her. *Yep,* she thought, *I am incompetent. I can't even make up any excuses at this point.* She hung her head, disappointed in herself and the fact that she looked like a big fool.

"I'm an idiot," was all she could manage to say and she sat on the floor. Liam sat down with her. She picked up the flashlight and started flashing it on the ceiling above. He was following the beam of light since there was nothing else to do or say at this point.

Finally Liam broke the silence, "No, you're not; just overwhelmed with a bunch of details, that's all."

"Maybe you can write me off on your taxes as a dependant," Charlie joked.

"Wait, what's that?" Liam said abruptly as he snatched the flashlight from her hand, pointing it toward a small panel above her front door.

"I have no idea."

"I need something to stand on."

She had nothing. The place was still empty; the furniture was another week away from delivery. He grabbed her mop bucket, turned it upside down, and climbed up on it.

The thought did not escape Charlie that the elegant Liam looked like he was standing on a pedestal.

The bucket allowed him just enough height to reach the door and open it.

"Well, there you have it. You have an electric card meter."

"What does that mean?" Charlie asked perplexed.

"Pay-as-you-go basically. It's a very old way of doing things. You won't be able to get a card until tomorrow at the store. This actually isn't your fault. The Letting Agency handling your flat should have briefed you on these types of details."

"Someone else handled this for me so they probably didn't pass on all the info. I will call tomorrow and see what else I should know. I am so sorry to have bothered you."

"Well, come on, we'll go back to my place. No reason to spend the night here with no heat."

"Liam, I couldn't possibly. Enough is enough, really. I am fine. You go home and enjoy yourself. Should I give you some money for the dinner?"

"Were did that come from?" he yelled.

"What do you mean?" Charlie said defensively also raising her voice.

"No. You don't owe anything for dinner. You were my date. I invited you."

He seemed angry. She had not heard this voice from him before and she didn't really like it. He was mad.

Irritated, Charlie snapped back, "Well I am so sorry, Sir. I didn't want to seem like I was taking anything for granted."

The door across the hall opened. Both their heads jerked to look. They had never shut the door and their yelling must have been echoing through the hallway. Charlie had not met her neighbors yet and she assumed now wasn't the right time. "Sorry," she was able to squeak out and the neighbor closed the door quickly.

"Get your things," it was an order. She didn't argue.

He must be so sick of me. I was his date.

72

CHAPTER 9

From the looks of his living room, Liam had been about to start a fire when she had called. Charlie found this odd because she thought he was going to do work which she assumed would have been at his desk upstairs. He went to the fireplace and started up the fire. She sat quietly on the couch.

"If you were going to steal money, how would you do it?" he asked out of the blue, somewhat grumpy.

"I don't know, how much money and from where?"

"We don't know from where, can't trace it anywhere, but we know it's not his and we can't really prove how he spent it."

"So how do you know he's got it? And who is HE anyway?"

"He is the guy we have been investigating. He is the only common link we have in this case."

"Well what kind of case is it?"

"We're still working on that too. We think it will be fraud."

"Well, how do you know you have a case?"

"The revenue department came to us because there were some discrepancies that they couldn't put their fingers on. So we looked into it. It led to some other companies and a few other people but this gentleman was the common denominator. He is linked to everything but there isn't anything but a lot of unexplained oddities."

"This makes no sense to me. Make him explain them."

"Well, that's the problem. If he knows we are looking into them then the trail might end. We don't want that to happen because we have had our eye on one company involved for years."

"Is he a bigwig?" she asked.

"Yes," he stated.

"I don't know, Dear."

He was sharing with her. This was a first. Her issues, her needs, and now he was bringing her closer, asking her opinion, perhaps even confiding in her.

She wished she knew the answer for him or could provide some new point of view that would stun and impress him but the details were too vague and her mind wasn't ordinarily a suspicious one to create motives and chains of events. All she could offer was an ear.

He rambled on about mistresses and huge pay raises, blackmail and money laundering. His mind was at work. *Liam. Liam.* She was staring at him. She felt the same as she had that day in the car – protected – and that made her feel relaxed.

Her mind wandered to yesterday morning when he woke her up and said, "Next time I won't knock. Noted – no pants." Her thoughts became racy as she pictured his long, toned legs intertwined with hers, his chest on hers.

"Are you even listening?" he questioned her sounding annoyed. She knew she was flushed. He had to know what she was thinking. It had to be written all over her face.

"Yes, except I don't know what any of it means." She managed to get out a coherent, well put-together sentence though in her mind, he was naked.

"Well, neither do I. So I guess that's that."

Seeing his frustration, she asked, "Do you want me to get you anything?" She prayed for something to do to shake this feeling that had come over her.

"No, I'm fine. Thanks anyway."

"I can see you have work to do, so please don't let me interrupt you. I can go."

Liam cut her off, "You need a phone or at least a cell phone. I'll take care of that tomorrow."

"Hold it now! I can do that, Liam. Contrary to what has played out over the past week, I am a capable woman," Charlie screamed.

"So you've said," he interrupted her. "I'm sure – actually positive – in America you are. But your track record here, Madame, is nil."

"That not true!," Charlie yelled, standing up for effect. "Besides handling all the crap at work, I have effectively utilized my resources – YOU!" Liam roared with laughter and took off after her. She squealed and ran but Charlie didn't know the house well and he caught her in seconds.

"Well, now that you have caught me," she said flirting but still squirming to get away, "what are you going to do with me?"

There was complete silence. *Now what?* She thought. She was excited. *Kiss me,* she silently prayed; *oh please kiss me,* she begged in her mind.

His hand left her arm and he touched her face lightly, sliding gently, slowly down her cheek. Charlie closed her eyes and tilted her face towards his fingers. When he reached the end of her cheek, he stopped and traced her lips with his finger. She wanted to open her mouth and provocatively suck on his finger but she was frozen. Normally not inhibited, she was out of her element. She feared that he didn't know her as the strong confident woman; that he knew her as almost helpless. She licked her lips unintentionally and he kept tracing his finger there. He hesitated in the center as if he wanted her to lick her lips again. Without thinking, Charlie parted her lips and teased his finger with her tongue. She expected him to withdraw but Liam didn't. He made his finger more available and touched the inside of her parted lips. She closed on the tip of his finger.

Liam thought he would expire. Her lips were so soft and warm. He never acted this way. He always maintained composure. He'd been to bed with models and even a TV personality or two and had never been affected as he was being now by this imp before him. Her tongue toyed with his finger and her head started moving, changing the depth of his penetration. *I want her NOW,* was his only thought. Self-control was quickly waning. *This madness must stop.*

Charlie's senses were consumed. She hoped he made the next move because her mind was not focused on formulating a plan; it was solely on how he was making her feel. She stayed the course, basking in the pleasure of the game. He shifted backward to kiss her forehead and withdrew his finger.

"There is only so much a man can take," he announced as he stepped away from her.

Charlie was embarrassed now. In the dark, she could hide but the light would bring a whole new dimension. Charlie said nothing, unsure of what avenue to take. She smelled fear. He was scared. She thought he must not have been out with a single soul since the lesbian betrayal. She was sure of it. The thought came that this could be her moment. Strong and assured, she could make love to him until he forgot everything else, everyone else. But what if he didn't want to? Why had he not tried? She was afraid she might scare him.

"I have half a mind to..." she quickly trailed off.

"Half a mind to what?"

Trapped by her own inability to control her mouth, she came out with it, "Half a mind to throw myself at you right now."

"Well, what's stopping you?" he challenged.

"Whatever's stopping you," Charlie whispered. He grabbed her. Pushing her hair away with both hands, he pulled Charlie's face up and kissed her. He crushed her to him and devoured her. Like two teenagers, they stood in the dark room and kissed. *I don't want this to ever end.* It was Liam who moved first, slowly pulling his head away but keeping his hands on her face. He finally took her hand in his and led her back into the living room. They sat on the couch quietly watching the fire, wrapped in each other's arms.

It was getting late. Charlie already knew she would be useless at work tomorrow with all this to think about. She needed to get some sleep. She should really get up and excuse herself. She also thought this must have been exhausting for Liam. She felt he had not ventured down this road in a while. Every superhero has an Achilles heal and this seemed to be his – a never-mended broken heart.

"Well, that's me off to bed, not that I really want to, but I am already going to be thinking about this all day tomorrow so I best not add tired and grumpy to my forthcoming concentration issues," she stated boldly.

"ALL day?" he flirted.

"Yep, and how I should have jumped ya!" Charlie jumped up with a laugh and ran upstairs.

I have no shame, she thought, *None!* She crawled into bed and wondered if Liam would know to get her up in the morning at the same time as before. She got up quickly and opened the door to tell him.

"OH! You scared me," she nervously announced pulling her shirt down. She hadn't even expected him to be upstairs yet. All she had on was her tee shirt that barely covered the essentials. "I wanted to make sure you'd get me up at 6:30 again."

"No problem," he said as he turned to leave.

"Well?" Charlie asked.

"Well what?"

"You were at the door, what was it you wanted? *Good one, Charlie, could you have not worded that different?* "I wanted to make sure you were OK and you are," he replied.

"And what where you gonna do if I had said 'No. I'm scared or need a bed time story'?" She was goading him, picking on him. She knew these were unfamiliar waters. She was exploiting his insecurity, but for the first time since they met, she felt in control.

"Well, what would you have done?"

"You are more than welcome to share my bed, Charlie, if that's what you want."

A wave of nausea immediately came over her. He said it in the most cold, uninviting way. He called her out and he won. She had pushed him too far. She was taunting him in his own house and he just slammed her to the ground. It was her own fault. There was no way to recover.

"Ouch," was all she came up with and turned back into her room, closing the door behind her. Crawling back into bed for the third time tonight, she wished the last three minutes away. He had kissed her and touched her tenderly. She was no idiot. She could read people. Slightly after midnight she thought, *I'll be OK with a few hours of sleep.* It was the cold she noticed. She hadn't been this cold last time.

The door opened slightly and a small beam of light shone in. Charlie sat up.

"I'm sorry," Liam offered, "That was uncalled for." He made his way over and sat on the edge of bed.

"Yes. It was," Charlie stated as she grabbed Liam's arm and lay down snuggling with it, hoping he would follow. He did.

"You are welcome to share my bed with me if you wish, but you must remain a gentleman," she chided.

78

"Smart ass," he chirped as he gathered her up in his arms and went to sleep.

CHAPTER 10

Friday

Liam was awake first. He watched her with her head on his bare chest, her olive skin next to his pale skin.

Charlie, he thought. *I am being undone by a loopy American. How can it be?*

He decided to wake her up. He knew she had on only a tee shirt. He slid his hand down onto her backside.

"YOU!" she blurted out, stunned by his advancement. She hurled herself on top of him. *Oh God! This isn't where I want to be,* as she tried rolling off. He held her there, "Well, now that you caught me, what are you going to do with me?" he teased.

"Very funny," Charlie conceded, "but you don't want to provoke me, Liam."

I will call you out on this bluff. While she was up there, she might as well torture him. She started moving. *A little dry grinding never hurt anyone.*

"You better stop," he warned.

"Or what?" she dared him.

"You never know."

"I'll take my chances" and she spread her hands on his chest. She was teasing him badly. She had no fear. He would never do anything. Liam lay there hypnotized as she continued to wiggle back and forth. Liam had enough. He flipped her onto her back and laid his full body weight on her. He began kissing her neck. Charlie's chest was pounding. Liam continued, her ears and then to her throat.

I was supposed to be calling his bluff not mine!

She had no idea that her own actions would be her undoing. She couldn't stand it any longer, "You win," she said defeated. "Please stop, I can't take anymore." The sound of her voice was a breathless plea.

"I can't," was all she heard him say. She thought of nothing but the smell of him, the feel of him, and as she started kissing whatever was closest to her, the taste of him. His hands were all over her. He whispered her name as his hands found her breasts and lower still. As he caressed her, she was gasping for air. She was writhing in the bed and he whispered words of encouragement. She clutched to his body as she trembled. Catching her breath, Liam gave her little time to recover and began kissing her again.

Her hands found him and with artful skill she stroked him. He fell onto his back, eyes closed to the pleasure Charlie was bringing him. He pulled her tight to him but her strong rhythm never stopped. "Liam," she moaned and that was all it took. He shook and growled until he had no breath left in him. She was amazed at the raw power he exuded. He was a man – a big man – and this was real.

Charlie was still held up tight next to his body. She didn't dare move. They were both sweating and the room smelled of lust. Her shirt had ridden up and her bare breast was touching his chest. It felt so nice. He cuddled her closer and Charlie put her arm over his chest. *I could get used to this,* she thought.

"I have to go to work, Liam," she said sadly, "not that lying here for the rest of the day isn't tempting." He kissed her and cupped her face with his hand. Charlie smiled down at him. "I'll drop you off," he offered.

Charlie got ready for work but Liam never left the bed. He watched her going in and out of the bathroom.

Finally when she came out, he was gone and the bed wasn't made. She quickly did so, then headed down the hall to his room and lightly tapped on the door.

"Come in," Liam called out.

In her usual sarcastic tone, "Ya know, the general rule is, lazy bones, the last one out of the bed makes it. I'll cut you some slack because I realize you have been out of the loop for a while." She flirted.

"And it's my house," he mentioned.

"Well, that too," she said embarrassed. His bedroom was dark. It had a huge dark cherry bed and matching dressing table. The carpet was deep red and a painting hung over the bed. Again, it was very manly.

As they got in the car, Charlie was giddy. He was a great guy. She had already met his mother and briefly his sister. *I wonder if this constitutes something. Are we dating? Is he my boyfriend?* To be on the safe side, she decided she better not make too much out of it. Liam pulled in front of her work.

As she was getting out of his car, she said, "I am cooking a decent meal tonight. You are more than welcome to come. I always cook too much anyway."

"I wish I could, Loopy but I have to work late again tonight. I'm sorry," he said sincerely.

"Right," Charlie said, hoping she didn't have one of those looks on her face. She felt uneasy about him declining her offer. She wished he had said 'yes'.

"No problem. Don't work too hard. Bye and thanks," she said, looking at the street. She closed the door and went into work.

It was Friday. She wondered what they would have done if it were a Saturday and neither of them had to go to work.

Adele had called and said a few friends were meeting for happy hour later but Charlie declined. A night in to sort through her thoughts was what she required. She fumbled through work. Her mind was on Liam – a big distraction. She couldn't concentrate on much. She addressed the staff and that was about it. She decided to go to lunch. Charlie took a long one, thinking it might clear her head.

Walking back into work, she wondered what Liam was doing. *I wonder if he will call me. I wonder when and if I'll see him again.*

She flopped into her chair. *What the hell is this?* On her desk was a wrapped box. She opened it slowly. A smile took over her face. There was a cell phone with a note on it and a number. The phone displayed one missed call. Charlie pushed the review button and the phone said Liam was the missed call. She played with the phone for a moment. The only number programmed into it was Liam's. Her smile grew wider. *He doesn't forget a thing does he?* She pressed 'send' and his line was ringing.

"Don't you think you have done enough for me?" she asked.

"Well I wanted to make sure you had no excuse not to call me."

"I see," Charlie replied.

"Plus," he added, "I need a favor." Just then her office door opened and there he was on his cell phone. Looking straight at him but continuing on the phone, "You got your one favor of the day this morning," Charlie teased. She was so happy to see him.

"I was afraid you were going to say that," sounding mockingly disappointed.

"Do you have good credit? Or perhaps we can work something out in trade?"

Liam hung up the phone and was standing before her. *My Lord, he is good looking.* Liam leaned in and kissed her. She leaned into the kiss ready to go for a few minutes when he pulled away. She squinted at him in confusion. Laughing at her puzzled look, "Relax. It's not like I'm never going to kiss you again."

"Well that's good news," Charlie said sarcastically. "And your favor?"

"Yes, my favor," he took a moment to compose himself. He seemed nervous. Something Charlie could never imagine him being. "There is a gala I must attend." And he stopped.

"That's mighty nice," she stated, "Have a great time."

"I'm not done yet!" he stuttered. "There is a gala I must attend and I was wondering if you would accompany me."

"That would be nice, I think." She was nervous because he was making such a big deal about of it. "What kind of gala is it?"

"It's a real fancy one with real snooty debutant types. Think you can handle it?" he challenged.

"I'm not sure if I am offended by that last statement. Are you implying that I am not ladylike enough to mingle with Scotland's finest?" Charlie's tone was daring.

"No, I'm not implying anything. I wasn't sure if that was your cup of tea," he answered defensively.

"So I would have to get a cocktail dress or an evening gown?"

"An evening gown. Do you not have one?" he asked, shocked.

"NO," Charlie answered with a snort, "Not too many people I know do have one just sitting in the closet."

"Well then we have a problem. The gala is tonight at 8 PM."

"Liam, you do realize for parties like this, women spend all day getting ready."

84

"I do now. I can buy you a dress," he stated, trying to convince her. "We can go now and get you one."

"Liam, most dresses have to be made and then fitted. Providing we find one I even like."

"No problem, let's go."

"You're high," she said, disgusted that he was that out of touch with reality. "No place can do that in six hours!"

"For me they can," he announced confidently.

"Really? And just who are you then?" Charlie asked with a real chip in her voice. He left her hanging for a moment.

Just who are you then? She wondered again about his big fancy house and how he had handled the matter for her with the bank manager.

"I'm someone to other people. I'm just Liam to you."

"So let me get this straight," sarcasm oozed from each word, "You're going to take me to get my hair done, you did mention that right?", Charlie asked with a wink not waiting for a reply. "And to get a dress, complete with tailoring, all by 7:30 so I can go to a fancy, high class gala with you, *that* everyone else knows about except me, your date, if I may be so bold as to call it that...a date"

"Yes, you are straight on the details. Are you in?", he asked impatiently.

Charlie picked up the phone. She called Mr. Moore and advised him she was leaving for the day and offered no explanation. She directed Roger to lock up and provided him with her new cell number should there be any issues. She turned to Liam, "I don't care who you are. This cannot be pulled off, but I am willing to get a hair cut out of trying." He opened the door for her and followed her out of her office.

CHAPTER 11

They got in his car and headed up Princes Street. She loved that street. She gazed at the castle. He drove farther down than she had been, and parked. To her right were six windows that displayed the most gorgeous dresses. Charlie began to get nervous. *I don't want him to know what size I am! This is going to be horrible.*

Liam had to buzz an intercom to be let in. He announced his name and a flawlessly dressed woman answered the door.

"Sir Liam – it's a pleasure."

"Thank you. We have a situation," he announced. He explained to the lady the time frame. She asked his budget. "Only the very best for the lady."

Charlie got chills when she realized that she was the lady. She was out of her league here. *Sir Liam? I guess Mr. is too common in a place like this.*

"Let's have a look at you." People descended on Charlie, poking, prodding, measuring, lifting, tucking and commenting. Liam was on the other side of the store speaking with another store representative. All at once everyone left her. She stood there. Liam glanced over and gave her a wink. Charlie decided to mosey through and have a look at some of the gowns. The price tags were enormous...£6500, £4300. *Holy Shit!* She hoped the sizes would be as big. Plus she needed hose, shoes – *I have no accessories!*

The lady who had answered the door came over. "Will you be wearing your hair up or down?"

"I don't know yet. I haven't gotten that far..."

"She'll be wearing her hair down," Liam interrupted.

"Down," Charlie repeated as though she had just made a decision.

"Will you be accessorizing with diamonds, pearls or jewels?"

"Pearls," Charlie began.

"Diamonds," Liam quickly corrected. Charlie's head snapped to him.

"I don't..."

"I know you love your pearls but tonight I want you to wear your diamonds."

"But I don't...." she started.

"I know," he stated authoritatively with a hint of understanding. *I don't have diamonds,* she said to herself. The saleswoman looked appalled at the pair.

Liam left. He said he would be back in 30 minutes. The lady returned, "Let's get this gown on you."

"But I have not picked out my gown yet."

"Sir Liam chose your gown."

"He what, I'm sorry?"

"He chose your gown." The lady repeated.

"I see."

Slipping the most elegant black gown over her head, Charlie found enough strength to ask, "You don't by any chance have anything..." as Charlie stuttered she was waving her hands over her trouble areas.

"A girdle?" the lady yelled.

Oh God! "Well, perhaps something that would help?" Charlie said with her eyes closed. *A girdle – thank God Liam was away.*

The attendants dressed her, pinned her, and helped her back out of the dress. It had only been an hour. *He is going to pull this off.* Charlie had no idea where to go for her hair or how she was supposed to rustle up some diamonds in the next five hours. As Charlie came out of the dressing area, Liam entered. "Are you through?" he asked with an "I told you so" melody to his voice.

"Yes, your Highness. I have to find a place for my hair."

"It's been arranged."

Charlie was dumbfounded at his response. *How would he know where to get hair done? Is that what he was doing? Making arrangements for my hair?* They got in the car and Liam drove her to a salon.

"When are you going to get ready?" Charlie demanded to know.

"Once you are squared away. Your appointment is under Marshall," he directed.

My appointment is under Marshall. This is not happening. This is a dream.

"Once I am done what do you want me to do?"

I will be back for you. And he left.

Walking into the salon, she was greeted by many people. Some seemed to be looking to see who she was as if they were expecting Angelina Jolie or someone far more exciting than Charlie Watson. She was handed a hot cup of tea and placed in a chair.

"My name is Stefan," the stylist said in a thick French accent. "I am the best in Edinburgh."

He was obviously gay and his antics where amusing as he spoke of what to do with her hair, the highlight tones and styles.

"It will look lovely," he finished. While Stefan worked the color into her hair, a manicure was underway compliments of the salon, she was advised. "How long will all this take?"

"You should be through by 6 PM and then the make-up artist will be here to finish your look." With his French accent and all the attention, it made Charlie feel far more posh than she had ever pretended to be in her life.

My look, she snickered. Her nails were finished in a lovely opal tone that she thought was going to look magnificent with her black gown. *I have never worn a gown. I hope I don't look like a stuffed pig and Liam is embarrassed to be seen with me in my girdle. Ahh – a girdle.* She was disgusted.

Time was ticking and more hair was falling than she wished to be cut but she had neither time nor right to speak up. At 6:15 PM she was spun around in her chair to look at Stefan's creation.

"Wow!" She couldn't believe it was her in the looking glass.

"You are stunning, Mademoiselle!"

She was. She was speechless. Her hair was shiny with red and blonde highlights around her face. She looked like a new person. Charlie was on top of the world. *Who cares about a girdle - I am beautiful!!*

The make-up artist decided to go for natural tones to compliment her olive skin. Jean-Claude praised her gorgeous skin the whole time he worked. By 6:45, all she could do was stare in the mirror. She looked like a movie star.

At 7 PM, Liam strode into the salon. He was dressed. Her mouth dropped open. His mouth dropped open too. They stared at each other for a moment taking in each other's transformation. Then they both tried to speak at once.

"You look amazing, Charlie!" he purred.

"You *are* amazing," she choked out.

"Are you ready for the ball, Cinderella?" he said tenderly.

"But I have nothing to wear," she joked lightly.

He took her hand and they headed out the door.

"Don't we have to pay?

"I already did."

"Liam?" He looked at her as they walked. "I've never been to a gala before," she confessed.

"I know – you'll do great. Don't worry."

"Liam?"

He looked again.

"Who are you?" she asked like a child.

"My mother's son" was the only answer she received. He held the car door for her and they went back to the dress shop.

Inside the store, people descended on her again. They were running around like chickens, waiting on her hand and foot. She was taken to a dressing chamber and the lady, whose name she was never told, handed her the girdle, stockings and a corset bra. It was awful. Moments later they slid the dress over her head, careful of her hair. Then shoes started coming at record pace. The dress felt good. It was comfortable but the shoes were not so kind. *How the hell am I going to walk in these?*

At 7:30, Charlie emerged from the back to a waiting Liam. He couldn't take his eyes off of her. She was stunning.

"You'll be the talk of the town, Charles!"

"Hey, only my dad calls me that! But I guess it beats Loopy. Are you going to tell me what type of Gala this is? Fair is fair."

"It's only 7:30. I have a half hour to spare and you said it couldn't be done!"

"Ok, you win, again, I might add," she said slowly, deliberately. He cast her a knowing look following her reference to this morning.

"We both won if I recall correctly," he stated without looking in her direction. Then he slowly turned to her, sharing his brilliant smile.

"You look gorgeous."

"Thank you."

The gala was at the Balmoral Hotel, right next door. He grabbed her hand as they walked. She had a shawl for the chilly night. Stopping short of the walkway to the Hotel, Liam said, "I almost forgot," and reaching into his breast pocket he brought out a small velvet box.

Charlie's eyes were glued. Liam opened the box slowly and it revealed the most dazzling diamond earrings Charlie had ever seen.

"Liam, they are gorgeous!" she crooned.

Teardrop diamonds, three on each strand, each about a carat, she guessed. He took them out and handed them to her to put on. She walked up to a window that she could use as a mirror, afraid that she would drop one of the precious jewels. She was wondering if he had bought them or borrowed them.

Reaching back into his breast pocket, he pulled out another longer box.

"You have got to be joking!"

This time there was a diamond necklace that shone in the street lamps, brighter than the North Star. He placed it around her neck. It hung across her chest and he fixed all the parts flat.

"Now, let's have a look at you. Perfect!" he said after taking a step back and giving her the once over. He presented his arm and she took it.

It can't get any better than this. A gorgeous man bearing gifts, I must be in a movie.

CHAPTER 12

They entered the magnificent hall and walked to the check-in table set up before a grand door.

"Sir Liam, so glad you could join us. Ma'am, a pleasure," the gentleman said, taking her hand and offering a kiss.

Charlie nodded with a sweet smile and a tilt of the chin, not knowing what the protocol was. Liam had been right - this was high class.

Don't talk much Charlie and you'll be ok. Open your mouth and you are in trouble.

Taking his arm once again, they entered through the ornate door. Everyone peered in their direction. Charlie was overwhelmed. She could smell the money that was in the place. Was he crazy taking her to this? *Can you handle it?* She remembered him asking. Now Charlie realized it was more of a dare.

She couldn't help but get the feeling that she was being used, not for sex and it certainly wasn't for money, but as though he had something to prove. She would enjoy herself for the evening and look into that later.

"Liam?" He looked at her. "Are we going to have to waltz and all that, because I don't know how to."

"I am a good lead, don't worry."

"Please tell me you are kidding? I do not want to embarrass you."

"You won't and you can't. Just be yourself. When I introduce you, use the same name I have said and you will be fine."

Charlie was introduced to earls and dukes, lords and dames.

I hope no one asks what I do for a living. I would die.

No sooner did that thought pass through her head did the question come from a young debutante who she would have sworn was flirting with Liam.

"I am on foreign assignment to orchestrate a multi-company merger."

Liam gave her arm a small squeeze and she thought she saw a glimpse of a smile. They moved on as the band struck up. "Ready for a whirl?

"Do we have to?"

"At some point, yes."

"Did my answer sound ok?"

"I was impressed; well done."

"Do these people even work?"

"No. Lots of old money here."

"And how did you get invited and what's the party for?"

"I am invited because I am a share holder in many of the businesses these people own. Plus a few other reasons including that the party is for Prince William."

"Prince William?" Charlie repeated astonished. "Will he be here?"

"Yes, he will be here."

"So, do these people assume I am someone, like you are apparently someone?"

"They probably will."

"I need to use the ladies room."

Liam escorted her to a hallway; he knew the place well. She entered the ladies room and looked in the mirror. She did look beautiful but she was out of her league. She was going to mess this up.

"Hello, I am Lady Elaine. I don't believe I know you." The lady was about 40 years old and held herself regally.

A pleasure, Lady Elaine, I am Charlie Watson.

"Charlie? A strange name for a girl. Is that a nick-name?"

"No, Ma'am," and she left it at that.

"And who are you here with?"

"I am here with Liam Marshall."

"You mean Sir Liam?"

"Yes, Sir Liam."

"Nice catch. How did you manage that?"

"I beg your pardon?"

"He is one of Britain's most eligible bachelors. Half of Britain has tried in the past two years to tie him into submission."

While saying this, Charlie felt the woman studying her up and down. Charlie had no answer. *Most eligible bachelor?* With a smile on her face and sugar dripping from her words, Charlie answered, "Ten minutes was all I needed." And she excused herself. She walked back down the hallway, her head held high and proud.

"Everything all right?"

"Why shouldn't it be, Sir Liam?" The sarcasm was evident. "Apparently I am here with one of Britain's most eligible bachelors. I was just told that half of Britain has been trying to tie you into submission for the past two years."

"Is that so," he said unaffected.

"So says Lady Elaine."

"Oh no – and what did you say?"

"I looked her straight in the eye and told her it only took me ten minutes!"

Liam let out the heartiest laugh. She had never heard him laugh like that before. She began to laugh too. The whole place was watching them laugh.

"Well done, Love, well done!" And he cuddled her to him.

The next hour was a breeze. People were in and out saying hello trying to get a glimpse of who she was.

94

Liam paid her many compliments. They danced a few times and she didn't muck it up.

"I will be back in a moment," he said. Charlie saw him go down the hallway toward the men's room. Two ladies approached her within seconds of Liam being out of sight. Both were stunningly gorgeous and for some reason, Charlie envisioned each with a role on The Guiding Light with their hair and makeup perfect even when they woke up in the morning.

"Well, I guess you are the pick of the litter this month," the blonde one said in a nasty attitude.

"I don't think so, Dear. I hardly return his calls," Charlie countered.

They snorted and promptly left. Looking around, she walked away slowly taking in all the details - the huge windows with their gaudy coverings, the chandeliers' sparkling crystals, the high ceilings with their ornate moldings.

"I hope you put them in their place"

"I'm sorry, what's that?" Charlie asked nervously.

"I said, 'I hope you put them in their place', the two who came over."

Charlie pursed her lips, not knowing what to say, puzzled that anyone even took notice of the exchange.

"I am Iain, Iain Mckenzie. I am a good friend of Liam's."

"Nice to meet you, Iain. I am Charlie Watson."

"Iain Mckenzie. I didn't know you were going to be here. I leave my girl for one minute and there you are sniffing around. You never change." Liam's jovial mood made pleasant banter between the old friends. Iain commented on the two who had come over and Liam's jaw tightened but he passed no comment.

The three of them talked and joked for a good half hour. Then Prince William arrived. A receiving line was set up and Charlie followed Liam to the back of the line. Overwhelmed by the notion she was going to meet and speak with Prince William, she started sweating. Not a real ladylike thing to do but she couldn't help it.

"Are you OK?"

"I don't know – I'm incredibly nervous to meet him."

"You will be fine."

"Liam, how are you?" Prince William said, hugging his friend.

"I am fine, Wills, just dropped in to support your cause. This is a good friend of mine, Charlie Watson."

Charlie didn't know if she was to bow, curtsy, or extend her hand. So she stood frozen like a moron. Liam gave her a small push to somewhat bow, which she did.

"It's a pleasure and an honor to meet you, Your Highness…"

William said the pleasure was all his to finally see Liam with a nice young lady. And he moved on.

"Thanks for leaving me hanging!!," Charlie said irately. "I couldn't call him Wills and you should have told me I was to bow."

"You did fine. Technically, you're not a British citizen so you didn't have to bow or curtsy."

"How does he know who you are? You hugged him, the prince, you hugged him!" she repeated, astonished by their familiarity.

"He is a family friend."

"He is?"

"Yes, do you care to dance again?"

"Not really, my feet are throbbing."

"So what did those two ladies say to you when they came over?"

"Why?"

"What do you mean 'why'?"

"I mean just that. Why? Why do you want to know? Who were they?"

"No games, Chuck, tell me."

"No, I won't. You've got your secret and now I have mine and gauging from the lock of your jaw when Iain said they came over, I assume correctly that it bothered you."

He dropped it, but, Charlie guessed, only for the time being. It did seem to bother him.

The rest of the night went smoothly. She met a few more people and Liam was very attentive to her. By 1:00 AM, they were walking to his car.

"Thank you for a very nice evening, Liam. I felt like a princess and you my charming prince. Not that I'm a big fairytale girl or anything. Wait till Ally hears I met Prince William and about this dress!! She will die when I tell her all about this."

"Who's Ally?"

"She is my best friend back home. I worked with her at my office in DC. I've called her a few times since I've been here. I really should call her more but I can only call from work and I don't want to take advantage of the phones there."

"Well, you can call her from my house."

"If I did that then I couldn't talk about you!," she said laughingly.

"So you talk about me? I see." He sounded as though he was a psychologist taking notes.

"I have mentioned you, nothing more, so don't get too excited," she joked.

"Well, thank you for being my lovely companion tonight. You were a charming date."

"Well, it cost ya, I'm sure. I saw the price tags on those dresses and it would be admirable if I offered to pay for it but I can't so I won't. But I do appreciate it; I have never been to anything like that in my life. I guess it's something a girl should do at least once in her life."

"Only once?"

"Well, I'm not really into that sorta thing. It's not something I would wish for over and over again. I'm a jeans, Diet Coke kinda girl, though nothing wrong with an expensive glass of champagne every now and then."

"I see," said the doctor again.

CHAPTER 13

The car ride home was short and she had expected him to drop her off at her apartment but he kept going to his place.

"Um, Liam? If I stay at your house, I have no clothes. Perhaps you should drop me off at my place?"

"I'm sure I will have something you can sleep in. It's just a tee shirt you require, I remember."

"Right," was all she could muster.

As they walked in, Liam gathered the mail from the floor. Charlie stood there, unsure of what to do. She had stayed all the other nights because of some crisis she had encountered. She always felt the invites were out of Liam's moral obligation to be kind. This was different; he actually wanted her here. He could have dropped her off without any repercussions but instead he kept her with him. On a Friday night – no work in the morning….she immediately became anxious. Her reasoning became filled with paranoia for unspoken expectations of what might go on the remainder of the evening.

"Let me see what I can rustle up for you." Liam disappeared up stairs.

I can picture myself here. In my glorious gowns, making scrumptious dinners in this kitchen, bringing him cups of tea as he works, sitting in front of the fire calling my family back home. Loving him. I could do that for the rest of my life.

"Here you are. One tee shirt," he announced proudly. He had changed as well.

"One tee shirt? So either we are going straight to ..." Charlie stuttered trying quickly to correct herself, "or rather, I am going straight to bed or I have to hang out with you here half naked. Hmm, decisions, decisions?"

He threw a pair of sweat pants at her with a wink. "Thanks." She walked carefully up the stairs to get changed. *I can't get out of this dress alone. Oh my God. I have a girdle on. And this corset. How am I going to get all those hooks undone? I need help. Oh my God. This is humiliating, what am I gonna do?* Charlie sat on the bed and was frantically searching for options. *I have no place to hide the girdle if by some stroke of luck I can get it off with the dress on. I have to try.* The girdle came right up under her breasts, then the corset, and the dress was fitted tight with the zipper still done. She couldn't reach over her head to loosen the zipper. She tried pulling the girdle down from under the dress. It wouldn't budge.

"Are you OK in there?" Liam asked as he lightly tapped the door.
"I don't know," she answered, distressed.
"Can I come in?"
"If you must."
"You haven't even changed yet. What's wrong?" He was puzzled.

Horrified, embarrassed, and exhausted, Charlie gave in to the truth. "I can't get out of the dress by myself."
"So I'll help. Why didn't you ask for help?"
"Because," she took a deep breath, "I'm embarrassed." Cradling her head in her hands with her eyes squeezed tight, she made her confession, "I have on ....a ...oh my god this is so embarrassing...I have on a girdle. I just want to die," she screamed in humiliation.

100

Liam laughed! "So what – half the birds in that place had one on."

Charlie squinted her eyes at him, not sure if he was telling the truth or just trying to make her feel better. Liam made his way to the back of her dress and unzipped it.

"Thank you, thank you. I can take it from here," she snapped before he tried to lift the dress over her head.

"Let me know if you need anymore help." With a wink, he closed the door behind him. It took her about fifteen minutes to get the dress off but she refused to let him see her standing there in the ridiculous thing.

"Thanks for your help," Charlie offered coming downstairs.

"That's what I'm here for."

"So, I didn't embarrass you at any point this evening did I?"

"Not once."

"Should I go out and take dance lessons so if this should ever happen again I can dance with other people?"

"As long as you go with me, there is no need for you to dance with other people."

"Ooh, is that…let me see...is that an order, a fact, a demand...not sure how to classify that answer. Sounded possessive too. I'll have to think on that."

"Allow me to spare you the time and effort. It was a fact."

"Noted," was her reply.

She joined Liam on the couch, wearing his tee shirt, no bra this time, and his sweat pants.

"I'll be up early tomorrow but I will be back by the time you are up and showered. I thought perhaps since the weather is mild we could go north for the day to a little place that has nice restaurants and quaint shopping."

Shocked by his preplanning, she replied, "Yeah, that sounds nice. I haven't been anywhere yet. But we'll need to run by my place so I can get some clothes."

"Well, you can either give me your key, tell me what you want and I'll get it on my way back or we can stop later, which ever you wish."

Surprised by his offer, she said, "Not sure. Let me think on it."

"You'd probably do well leaving a few things here for situations like these."

"What?," Charlie asked, stunned by what she heard him say.

"You should probably leave a few things so you aren't always caught with nothing here."

Charlie gazed at him in utter confusion.

Men don't tell women to leave their belongings at their home; it cramps their style or makes them feel as though there is a relationship. Makes them feel pressure and all that Dr. Phil bullshit.

"Let me get this straight. You WANT me to keep stuff here?"

"Well, it makes the most sense. You've spent four nights out of seven here and we always have to stop at your place to get your work clothes."

"I really need to call Ally," she muttered. Liam was puzzled. He had no idea why he had said it but it seemed natural for him to say it. He has had this woman in his bed and he hadn't even bedded her yet. What was he waiting for? He knew he could. She was his constant companion and he was thankful the tabloids had left her alone thus far. But after tonight's coming out, he knew it was inevitable – perhaps even tomorrow

102

morning her face would be all over The Mail. So far she'd not asked for an explanation of what they were doing and he wasn't ready to give one so he figured *let a sleeping dog lie.*

"You can use the phone in my office if you wish."

"No, thanks. I also need a pack of cigarettes and a glass of merlot for this phone call."

"You smoke?" he asked surprised.

"Occasionally. When I am stressed or drinking. Or feel like being bad. And don't throw your nose up at me, I can smell the cigars upstairs from your office."

"Anything else I should know?"

"Not that I know of, but I didn't know that was something you needed to know anyway. Besides there are a few things I know you haven't told me, so don't you dare throw the first stone, SIR LIAM."

Liam answered with a thrust of his wrist in a touché manner acknowledging defeat. "Well, if you want a cigar, they are up there."

"Matter of fact, I think I will…If you want to be shocked, Liam, I can do that easily."

Charlie sat confidently in Liam's high-backed leather executive chair, an unlit cigar in her fingers; her feet up on the desk, and the phone perched to her ear.

"Ally, I don't know what to make of it. No, I'm here at his house. I'm using his phone. He's down stairs."

Ally's quick strain of questions confirmed to Charlie how bizarre the whole situation was. She went on to explain the gala, the gown, the jewels, spending the night, the offer to keep clothes there, his day planned for them tomorrow, the whole thing - nary a detail was left out.

"So why are you telling me all this? You are savvy enough to see what it all adds up to," Ally responded.

103

"Well, that's the thing, Al, if all he was after was sex, for one he would have tried by now and two he would be keeping me on my turf not his so it's easier to walk away once he gets what he wants. It's almost as if he really likes me."

"And what's wrong with that? You deserve a nice guy. Why can't you have a nice guy for a change?"

"Because all of this is all too fairytale for me and you know I don't believe in that bullshit! Plus he won't tell me who he is, if he *is* something, but The Prince knew him and they hugged. So I have to say he is someone and the ladies said he was the most eligible bachelor. He could have any woman he wanted. All he has to do is call and they'll be there, I am sure, with bells on. So why would he want me?"

"Maybe 'cause you're not like all of them? Play it cool – make him earn it. Perhaps he wants you more than you know. Lead him around a little. Check out what he's made of."

"Maybe I will. I'm not the game-playing kind but he is playing a game, isn't he. 'I'm my mother's son'…what kind of game is that?"

After an hour of chitchat, Charlie was tired. It was closing in on 3 AM. Liam never disturbed her.

Coming out of the office, the downstairs was dark, so she assumed he had gone to bed. His bedroom door was closed.

She waltzed into her room, remembering the waltz they had danced and reflecting on the night's events. It had been a great night. She took off the sweat pants and crawled into bed only to plop right on to Liam.

"OUCH," he yelped

"What the hell are you doing here?"

"Well, I wanted to know what your precious Ally told you but I was tired. No pants…"

"Stop that! Get out of here," she said half joking, praying he wouldn't leave.

Moving over to make room for her, he asked again, "So what did Ally say?"

"Thank you for letting me use your phone."

"Don't change the subject."

"I didn't, we didn't talk about you."

"Liar."

"Are you staying in here?"

"Yes."

"Good night then." And she rolled on her tummy and got comfortable.

His leg came over her feet. "I guess we'll be collecting your clothes together."

"You can take my key. Grab me a pair of jeans, any sweater and my sneakers."

"Trainers."

"Who?"

"Not 'who', 'what'…we call them 'trainers'."

"OK then, my trainers."

"Can I look through your underwear drawer?" he said, teasing her.

"I don't have ANY drawers yet and besides, I don't wear underwear," she said into her pillow, annoyed because she was trying to sleep.

"See, that was one of those 'anything else I should knows' that you didn't tell me."

"Well, now you know, more than I can say from you, SIR LIAM."

He softly snorted. Even tired, her mind was sharp.

CHAPTER 14

End of November/Beginning of December

It was apparent no effort was being made to replace Mr. Duval. Work was being sorted and the new receptionist was becoming familiar with the routine.

Charlie was coming to terms with the fact that she was flying solo. As she struggled to keep the company moving and more importantly moving forward, it began to gnaw at her that she was having to do this with no guidance.

I'm being taken advantage of; I think I deserve a raise! This has significantly reduced their payroll plus now they are getting 3-for-1 labor between Mr. Duval's duties, Will's accounts that I am handling, and my own responsibilities.

Getting herself all wound up, she picked up the phone, "Mr. Moore," and Charlie began to build her case. After 35 minutes, Mr. Moore saw the light and Charlie received a $25,000 raise retroactive to when she arrived 2 months ago. She felt empowered. She called Liam to tell him the news.

"Excellent, Loops! Should we go out tonight and celebrate? Your treat of course," he teased.

"Sure, that's a great idea. What do you have in mind?"

Liam suggested a new high-class bar called The Silver Dollar in the city center.

Charlie had heard talk in the office of The Silver Dollar. "We can't get in there. It's basically private and then you have to leave at 10 PM if you're not on the VIP list."

"Don't worry. I'll sort it," he replied. Charlie believed him. He would get them in.

After work, Charlie got all dolled up and was shocked when Liam arrived at 7 PM, earlier than she had expected. As always, he was dressed perfectly and looked magnificent.

"Well, look at you!" he said.

"It's new. You like?" Charlie said, motioning and twirling in her new dress.

"I like," he simply said.

Catching up on the day's events, they sat in the elegance and trendiness of the bar that Charlie thought to be more suited to NYC. Liam had ordered a bottle of fine champagne and teased about the last time a woman bought him champagne. Again, people seemed to take note of them.

"Liam," Charlie gained his attention and questioned, "Why is everyone so intrigued with you?"

"Because they have nothing better to do," he declared.

"I've been good here, Lee." It was a mark of their new intimacy that she was calling him Lee from time to time. "I've not asked too many questions or pestered you. I didn't go on and on about what the ladies said at the gala. But I have to tell ya, sometimes I feel like when I go to the store that I need to glance at the tabloids to make sure I'm not on the front page. We've been friends for nearly two months. I don't care what answer you tell me, you will still be Liam. But I want YOU to tell me, if not, I'm gonna give up and Google you," Charlie threatened.

"I thought you would have by now and that's why you've not asked."

"No, I haven't. I want you to tell me," She repeated.

"I'm no one really. I have a fancy title at work, a little clout in the government and I'm single. That's all people need to start running," Liam confessed.

"I don't believe you but it's a start."

The bubbly was excellent and she had three glasses to his one. He ordered another bottle.

"Would you come over for dinner on Friday night? I'm making my favorite dinner that my mom normally makes for me - Barbeque beef over rice. Love the stuff!"

Charlie was lazing in her chair, getting flirty with him. He recognized she was getting tipsy. He agreed to come.

"You promise? It's only two days away and if you can't come I want to make other plans. I refuse to spend my birthday alone," she announced.

"Your birthday?! How come you never told me?" Liam seemed annoyed.

"Well I'm telling you now," she said, refilling her champagne glass. She felt good. They danced to a few songs, something Charlie never did. She always said, "I can move my top or my bottom but not both at the same time in any way respectable for public viewing."

At 1:30 AM they grabbed a cab and headed home. Charlie fell asleep cuddled into Liam.

The 6:30 AM wake up came early and Charlie was very confused by Liam waking her up. Dazed, she sat up, looked around, and then back at him. "What happened?" Her voice was rough with sleep.

"Nothing. You fell asleep in the cab. I wasn't about to look through your purse for your keys, so I brought you here," he explained. Charlie didn't remember changing. She was only wearing one of his tee shirts and she was in his bed, not her normal room.

"I'm ill," she announced, flopping back into the pillows and pulling the duvet over her head.

"A bottle and a half of champagne has been known to have that effect on people. But you have to go to work. You received an enormous raise and it wouldn't look good." He was right. "I'll run the shower for you."

Stumbling down the stairs in last night's clothes, she saw Liam crack a smile as he handed her coffee.

"I'm a mess," she proclaimed.

"You'll be all right. Here." She ate the toast he had made.

Liam drove to her apartment where she quickly changed and went off to a long, arduous day of work. Every task was twice as hard to perform and Charlie swore she would never drink again. When lunchtime arrived she opted for a nap at her desk. Her cell phone rang.

"Hello?"

"How are you feeling," he questioned.

"Lee, it's horrible. I'm taking a nap. Please don't ever let me drink again."

Laughing, Liam replied, "No, no. That's on you. I'm not getting involved. Is there anything you want me to bring for tomorrow night?"

"Just you, my dear. That's enough."

"All right. How about I come right after work so I can see how you make this favorite meal of yours?" he asked.

"Sounds good to me."

"Ok then. I'll see you tomorrow. I'm working late again tonight."

The second half of the day was just as long and painful as the first. Five o'clock arrived in the nick of time. Charlie thought she was about to die. Wanting nothing more than to go home and sleep off her sore head, she knew she had to go to the butcher for tomorrow's dinner.

Harrison's Butcher Shop was well acclaimed in the Tollcross area of Edinburgh. Everyone knew if one were on this side of town, there was only one place to go. Passing the shop every day on her way home from work, Charlie was familiar with the lines pouring out the door. It was a special meal and only the best would do. Charlie was finally going to the butcher.

It's your own fault, Charlie, you feel this way. You know better! You are not a drinker.

Her lecture certainly wasn't making standing in line any easier. Not to mention that the smell of the meat was turning her stomach. *A pound of stew beef, Charlie, and then get yourself home.*

Each woman in front of her seemed to be ordering enough meat to feed a small underdeveloped country. *If I wait in this line and there is no stew beef left...*

The lady directly in front of Charlie had her list. The list seemed to be comprised of each day's meals through the weekend. *Is the butcher closed on the weekend? Is everyone ordering meat for the WHOLE weekend?* One by one orders were filled and packaged. Thirty minutes later, she listened to the crumpled list of the woman before her. "I'll have 450 grams of mince, 250 grams of black pudding, 250 grams of white pudding..." *Grams? What the hell is a gram? How many grams in a pound?*

"Miss, what can I get for you?" Charlie stared at the man before her with his paper white hat and blood stained apron. "Miss, are you ready to order?"

"Umm, I, ahh," she stammered. The man was looking between her and the rest of the line waiting behind her. The hurry up gesture only made matters worse.

110

"I...I would like a pound's worth of grams of stew beef please," said the American accent. Charlie felt the heat in her face. *I'm an ass.*

"Don't worry, Lass, we only changed over to grams a wee while ago. There are 454 grams in a pound. I'll get yer stew beef for you," he said politely.

"Thank you." Charlie managed a smile even though she felt as raw and dumb as the side of beef she saw hanging behind the glass window.

Friday arrived. Her birthday. She had already received a card from her parents. Her nieces and nephew had made her special cards as well. Charlie was well rested and had a spring in her step. She was excited about tonight.

"Charlie?" the voice of the new receptionist came over the intercom. "Yes, Louise?"

"You have a delivery here in reception." Charlie came out of her office to the most gorgeous two dozen red roses she had ever seen.

"Are they from Liam?" Louise inquired.

"I sure hope so. I don't know anyone else," Charlie laughed. She grabbed the card: 'Happy Birthday to my special funny bone. XOXO, Liam'. Charlie reread the card. *'Special funny bone'?*

Charlie brought the arrangement into her office and called Liam. " 'Your special funny bone'? What's that mean?"

"You make me laugh, Charles. That's what I love most about you."

"I see, well, thank you very much. They are gorgeous. Thank you."

That's what he loves most about me? The thought kept repeating through her head.

A wave of nausea overcame Charlie at the possibility that he changed her into his tee shirt last night while she was drunk and not sucking in her stomach. She didn't want to know. At least this way there was a shadow of a doubt, a possibility that she unknowingly got changed herself. All she could do was cringe when the thought entered her mind. *She'd have to get over it,* she told herself.

Charlie made her list of what she needed at the store for tonight's dinner. She tortured herself over what to wear and she felt all giddy with excitement. *Perhaps he'll stay at my place tonight.* This could prove interesting since they had never stayed at her place before. All morning her thoughts were occupied with tonight's events. It had been a while since he had kissed her.

Charlie decided to go to lunch early and pop into the wine merchant for a good bottle of merlot to accompany her meal. She laughed at herself. She had only made the promise not but 24 hours ago to never drink again and already she was reneging. Turning the corner Charlie froze. The tears came and her mouth gaped open. She was stunned. Her legs felt like concrete and her hands were shaking. She couldn't believe what she was seeing. Walking toward her arm and arm with a beautiful blonde woman was Liam. She couldn't catch her breath. Charlie started walking backwards in retreat but never taking her eyes off the painful sight. She was devastated. It was then that Liam saw her.

"Charlie," he yelled but she turned and ran. Her breathing was labored. She felt like she was going to throw up.

"Charlie! Wait!" Liam continued to yell. He had seen her face. He saw the disbelief. He began to run after her. Charlie ran into the shopping center and went out another exit.

I can't believe I could be so stupid, she cried to herself. She walked many blocks, not knowing where she was going, all the while crying, sniffling and hurting. *Why did I believe there was something there? Why did I believe that I could be enough for a man like him? You're so stupid, Charlie!*

It hurt. She wanted to go home, back to Maryland. She never wanted to see Edinburgh again. As she sat in some seedy bar, eyes red and puffy, she tried reasoning with herself. *What did you expect? We aren't an item. He never said I was his girlfriend or that we were exclusive. I mean we aren't even sleeping together.* Again, the vision of this morning popped into her head. She ordered another vodka tonic.

Four hours and several vodka tonics later, she was sitting in a corner booth with three dudes reeking of beer, hanging all over her. Not high-class dudes by any stretch of the imagination, not one of them had many teeth.

"Ach, Hen, if I had a bird like you," one was saying. She was disheveled and her mascara was down her face but she was too drunk to care. She was hurt enough to crave any distraction.

"See you, Lovey. I'd treat you like a queen!" another offered.

"Excuse me," a voice came, "Come on - you're coming with me!"

"Like Hell I am, Liam! Leave me alone. Go back to your blonde. Leave me alone!" Charlie was screaming.

Liam was pulling on her arm and she was shrugging him off.

"I have new friends now. Tell'm boys!" she slurred, but not a word was spoken. She looked up at her three toothless wonders and they all were looking at Liam like he was a celebrity.

"What good are any of ya worth!?," Charlie yelled in hatred.

Liam picked her up, threw her over his shoulder, and walked out gracefully.

"Put me down, you asshole! You fucking asshole – I hate you – put me down!!"

"Well, if you want to get on the cover of one of those tabloids, you are doing a great job," he said calmly. That shut her up. He hailed a cab.

Once inside the cab, Charlie tried to get out the other side but he snatched her.

"You will stay in this cab and you will ease up on your language," he ordered in her ear. He held her so tight there was no way she would be able to get out.

"Get your hands off me. Don't ever touch me again!" she snarled, keeping her voice low. He ignored her and her request. Liam threw some money at the driver, never lessening the firm grip he had on her until they were in her apartment.

"I can't believe you did that to me, you asshole, and on my birthday! If you had a girlfriend, you should have told me. Now I feel like a fool thanks to you. Get out of here, get out!" she screamed, pushing him toward the door while pounding on his chest.

Liam let her have her say then he grabbed her arms to her side. "That's enough!" he bellowed. Charlie stopped for a brief moment, long enough to glance at his face, which held a look she didn't recognize. She was still crying. He forced her back into the living room and onto the couch.

"That was my sister," he said calmly, "Again, they cause me bother, don't they? She is a travel agent. She brought me the two tickets that I purchased yesterday to Italy."

He threw the tickets on her lap. "I was walking her back to the train station," he finished.

Charlie picked up the tickets and looked through them. One had his name and the other hers. She didn't know what to do. She buried her head in her hands and cried, more with relief than anything else, she was sure.

"I am sorry, Charlie," he offered, "I wish you would have stopped and the whole mess would have been cleared up in seconds."

Charlie couldn't speak. Not only was she embarrassed by her behavior, she was mortified at what he must be thinking. She had played it so cool with him, never letting on how deep her feelings were. Taking a second to regroup, she thumbed through the tickets.

"This plane leaves tonight!" Charlie snapped to attention,

"Yes, I know. That is why I searched high and low for you until I found you. So hurry up! Get your stuff, you have five minutes. Whatever you don't have we will buy."

Charlie sprang into action snatching anything and everything she could - makeup, jeans, slacks, blouses, shoes, you name it. Five minutes were very short and Liam announced, 'Time's up'.

They grabbed a cab to his place where he picked up his already-packed case. He was back in the cab in seconds and headed to the airport. There was silence. Charlie's head hurt as the vodkas began to wear off. She had no idea what to say. No one had ever done anything so extravagant for her. He must feel so slighted by her unspoken accusations.

"Don't worry about it Chuck," he said as if he were reading her mind. "Let's have a nice three days in Italy."

"Three days? I have to work on Monday."

"No you don't. It's a bank holiday."

"Really?"

"Really."

CHAPTER 15

What a surprise all this was. She was going to have to bring it up eventually, if he didn't. What was she to say? *I thought you were cheating on me?* They never spoke of a relationship. *I thought we had something going on?* That would be too assumptive.

Liam grabbed her hand as their journey started. "So where exactly are we going?" she asked.

"First, we fly into Catania, Sicily. Then we have a 50-minute ride to Taormina. It's a quaint seaside village with a lovely walk looking over the sea."

"Thank you, Liam. This is very nice and unexpected," she said sincerely.

"Happy Birthday." He squeezed her hand.

"Won't we be getting there very late?"

"Yes, but I have made all the arrangements for a car to pick us up. We'll be fine."

"I'm sorry to bring this up, Liam. I just want to get it out of the way so it doesn't hang over me this whole trip. I don't know why I reacted that way. I had no right to, I know. I certainly don't need a lecture on that but it hurt just the same. I'm truly embarrassed for, for...." she stuttered, knowing she had backed herself into a corner and now had to admit she cared for him more than she let on, "...for not being truthful with myself about being able to handle a platonic male relationship."

Her whole speech was done with her eyes closed. When she finally opened them, Liam was staring at her.

"What are you saying?" he asked baffled.

"I don't know, I guess," she was mortified. *What do you mean what am I saying? Don't you know how hard it was for me to say what I said and now you want me to explain it better?*

Charlie didn't even want to ask simple questions like the length of the flight or the weather in Italy. Not even the one question that was burning in her stomach, precisely, 'what are the sleeping arrangements?' She decided by the time they got there, she would be so tired she probably would sleep on the floor and not mind.

As she sat silently, she slowly realized - *A quaint seaside village.... that's a place where lovers go. Italy, that's a place where lovers go too.*

"So what time do we land?" she chirped with excitement.

We will get into Taormina about midnight. They are an hour ahead of us. We are staying in a beautiful hotel called Isola Bella – it means beautiful island.

"I can't wait," she stated as her stomach growled. "I hope they at least give us some peanuts. I'm starving."

"This is first class, Loops. You can have whatever you want. May we have a bottle of champagne please?" Liam politely asked the steward attending their cabin.

"Does champagne go with a vodka tonic hangover?" Charlie whimpered.

"I guess you will find out. But I'm not holding your hair in the toilet should you get sick   there's only room for one in there."

After two glasses of champagne and a good meal, Charlie was sleeping on Liam's arm. Never having been in first class before, she had drifted off to sleep telling herself that this had ruined her for coach travel for the rest of her life.

"Wake up, Loops – we are landing in 20 minutes."

"How long have I been asleep?"

"About 3 hours."

"Sorry. I guess I'm not a very good travel companion, but at least my hangover is gone."

She couldn't see much out the window. A few lights, but nothing looked very populated. Charlie got really excited and nervous. *As soon as we get there it will be time to sleep.*

Liam collected their luggage then caught sight of a limo driver holding a sign that said, 'MARSHALL'.

"That's us, Chuck."

The limo was sleek, not like the wide American vehicles she knew limos to be. It had a bar that Charlie vowed to ignore.

Crawling in, Liam sat next to her and grabbed her hand. "Are you ready for a nice birthday?"

"It's already been great, even if we went home now! I can't imagine it getting any better."

The streets were very old and narrow. The towns were silent and still. She felt they were the only two people awake in the world. The coastline was directly on their left and a few lights dotted the horizon.

"I can't wait to see this place in the day. It's looks magnificent even at night!"

The limo pulled down a gravel road that unveiled a huge hotel overlooking the water - Isola Bella Bay.

"Liam, look at this place. Oh my God, it's unbelievable. I don't think I even packed a camera." The hotel overlooked Isola Bella, a beautiful island with a castle ruin surrounded by water on three sides. Smiling wide and blinking her eyes to make sure it was all real, she was speechless at its beauty in the dark. *I wonder what the daylight will bring.*

Liam helped her out of the vehicle and tipped the driver. A valet came for their bags. The wonderful feeling of Italy engulfed her as she walked into the hotel. She could sense the slow paced, genuine love of being alive, the smells of good food, history and pride. Her shoulders instantly relaxed.

Three days to go. I never want it to end. After her nap on the plane, she was hardly tired. She was invigorated. Charlie wanted to explore everything. She didn't want to wait until morning.

Their room was everything that one could imagine. There were rich, heavy fabrics with bold colors of blue and yellow. The private bath had enormous windows with a clear view of the sea. There was one huge bed, so lofty that it had steps.

Well that answers that question.

Charlie instantly became scared. Her thoughts scattered. *He is older. Oh my god, I forgot to shave my legs!*

Gathering her composure, Charlie announced, "This room is gorgeous!! Thank you Liam," as she bowed her head hoping he couldn't read her thoughts.

"Don't thank me, thank my sister. She is the one who made all the arrangements – I've never been here before either. It is beautiful isn't it?" he said, looking around.

The incident about his sister seemed years ago but in truth it was only hours ago. Charlie decided to let it go. She had different worries now. Liam tipped the valet and they were alone.

Charlie's nerves started. In quick rapid-fire chatter, she erupted, "So have you researched where to go, what to do? What was this walk you talked about? How far away is it? Can we walk there? Do you think they have a good gelato place here? I think they will, I mean it is Italy and all. I've seen a place like this on the travel channel and they make these pottery number plates for your house...."

Liam threw her on the bed and started kissing her. "Let's get this over with so you can relax."

There, he had said it. He kissed her until he felt her give in. She didn't have the time or the energy to think about all her worries. All she knew was Liam was making her mind scrambled with pleasure and Charlie wanted more. He got up and closed the light. Only a bright moon shone through the windows while he undressed. Charlie's eyes were fixed on the scene playing out before her. There was no guessing what was to go on at this point and there was no running away either. As Liam climbed back on the bed, he started to undress her – slowly and with great pleasure – he took his time, he was in no rush.

When they had arrived, she had wanted to explore everything - at that time this wasn't what she was thinking.

Naked, Charlie looked into his eyes. They were intense. The normally laid back, calm Liam seemed focused and serious. His hands never left her body. His mouth kissed her lips then her neck. Charlie let out an audible breath. Encouraged, Liam paid close attention, enjoying her response to his touch. Charlie was desperate to feel him. She caressed his back, took in his scent, and moved in rhythm with his tongue. His hands rolled down her stomach and reached down the length of her thigh. Charlie wanted to explore him. She nipped at his ear and kneaded his chest. He leaned up on his arms and Charlie began kissing his chest. She wrapped her arms around his waist and towed her tongue downward. Feeling him tense, she brought her hand around and traced from his belly button lower and still lower. He went to his knees freeing his arms. She took him in her hands. Charlie felt his neck snap back in pleasure. He was ready for her but she wanted to know him. Liam's response was all the encouragement she needed. She didn't cease, her pressure increased, faster and harder feeling his short, quick breaths. Liam snatched her head and pulled her mouth away from him. In the same move he devoured her lips and laid her on her back. His knee pushed her legs apart and he bore down on her. She arched her back and groaned as he came into her. His rhythm was strong and needy. Every stroke was deeper. Charlie moved in sync with his every move, eager meet him, until finally, together, they collapsed.

Their languid bodies lay naturally together. No words were spoken as each tried to breath steadily. Liam moved to his side and pulled her closer to him. He kept his arm around her as they fell asleep... sated.

Liam awoke first. He looked at Charlie, still sound asleep, and wondered how such a real person could exist in this world. He didn't think she had any idea what she did to him, how she made him laugh with her antics and how much he missed her when she is not there. Her antics, he thought, deserve a sitcom. She is so real. There is nothing fake about her. She is appreciative and doesn't expect anything from me.
But, that is because I have not told her who I am. I am so unfair. She probably won't want me once I tell her. I have to tell her. Not telling her is nothing short of a lie. I am a liar.

His mood changed from happy and optimistic to anger - at himself for being a coward. Charlie stirred and opened her eyes to see Liam scowling down at her. Her eyes went to a panic instantly thinking he regretted what they had done.
Are you OK, she worried, blinking at him.

"I have been unfair to you. I'm sorry. I am a coward."

"Unfair? How?" Deep concern rang in Charlie's voice. "How are **you** a coward? You are always my hero!" She smiled.

121

"Because I wouldn't tell you who I am or who people think me to be. I loved knowing you wanted to be with me because it was just me and not everything else."

"What is everything else?," Charlie questioned as she sat up, holding the covers over her. Liam could see the worry and fear on her face.

"People think it's important that I am the godson of the Queen. My mother is the Queen's niece. Therefore I am also the Queen's nephew. I have worked hard my whole life and not fallen back on that. I wanted to prove my own worth. And I did, but the tabloids love it and have a field day with it. I am wealthy because I earned it, not because I have inherited some of it. And the ladies, well you can't tell which ones are real and which ones are fortune hunters who want to go to balls and buy pretty dresses and be handed costly jeweled baubles."

"What's a bauble?"

"Jewelry and hair things. I don't know - it's an old fashioned term," Liam said, confused at her idiotic question.

"So that's it? That's the big secret you have held from me? Do you realize how scared you just got me? I thought you were going to tell me you had AIDS, or you had six months to live or you were on trial for murder and I'm stuck in a foreign country with no way to get home. You're a rich kid! So what!"

Charlie stormed from the bed into the bathroom and slammed the door. Liam sat stunned by her reaction. With a towel wrapped around her, Charlie came charging out of the bathroom like a bell had rung for round two in a boxing match. "And let me tell you something else, Little Lord Fauntleroy, I don't want nor do I need your money if that is what you are worried about. I too make my own way in life. I will earn my own baubles, thank you very much, I am not much of the princess kind – if you haven't noticed – I have a hot temper and don't enjoy having to bite my tongue – so not only have you wasted your time, you have wasted mine. I can't be part of your society nor do I want to be. This is going to be a long three days! I wish you had told me this in the beginning so I could have run so far and so fast, but now I..." Charlie stopped, breathless, staring at him with agony on her face.

Liam looked at her amazed. "But now what?"

Charlie couldn't hold back her tears. They began to drain slowly out of the corner of her eyes. She was trapped by her heart. With her head looking at her bare feet on the floor, she simply said, "but now I ....I ....need you. I don't even know your middle name and yet all I do all day long is think about you. I think about how I feel so safe with you and you think I'm funny and you don't yell back when I fly off the handle. I almost feel you think that is charming! You do, don't you?" Slowly she looked up at him and went on again.

"Because I don't conform to any of that bullshit, do I? Here I thought I was taking advantage of you and your kindness because I was so needy with all my mistakes but really you were using me. I would never know who you were and therefore you could see if someone would really like you for you. It all seems so clear to me now. Again, I say to myself, *What would you want with a girl like me? – I should have known better.*"

Charlie gathered some clothes and got washed and dressed in the bathroom. She exited and went straight out the door. She didn't even know if Liam was still there.

CHAPTER 16

She felt like she had walked forever. The road up from the hotel was steep and because of last night's escapade, every sore step was a dagger reminding her of her stupidity. She yelled at herself to get a grip but the truth was there and couldn't be ignored. She loved him. Everything about him, his walk, and the way he read the newspaper. Everything. So many ironic things went through her head. Like when they had arrived and she never wanted the three days to end and now she wanted to go home. Liam thought his secret was more of a gift when in fact it was like a piece of coal at Christmas.

The views were breathtaking and she did wish Liam were there to share them with her.

How did he expect me to react? Like I had hit the lottery?

Finding her way up the hills to the *passigita*, she walked and watched. There was a light breeze but nothing too chilling that her small coat didn't protect. There were artisans painting, musicians playing, people strolling and Charlie sulking. *This isn't my fault!*

Charlie found a small outdoor café. She bought a cappuccino and sat overlooking the sea.

I love him, so now what do I do?

She couldn't call Ally.

The smell of the sea and the warmth of the sun didn't do anything to inspire her thoughts. They only made her more morose. Pity was something all too familiar these past few months and she was sick of feeling it. Up so high one hour and down so low the next. *The emotional roller coaster he has me on is gonna kill me.*

'Loops', 'Charles', 'Chuck' – all the names made her feel cherished. He made her feel that way. *I can't be that wrong, can I? He has to feel something for me, doesn't he?*

She sipped the next two cappuccinos, lost in deep thought. Noon was fast approaching and although the day was creeping by, something had to be done. They can't spend three days ignoring each other nor two nights. *Nights. I would enjoy two more nights like last night.*

"Is this seat taken?"

Charlie raised her face to see Liam standing guiltily before her. She closed her eyes and motioned for him to take a seat.

"I'm in love with you Liam. What do you suppose I do now?"

He had never heard such glorious words in all his life.

"I don't deserve it, but I have never been so happy as to know someone like you would ever love someone like me. You have no idea what an incredible human being you are, how honest and sincere you are. You have no idea what you do to me and for me." By the time Liam was done his speech, he was on his knees cupping her face looking directly into her eyes.

She leaned down and kissed him.

As they walked through the passigita, holding hands in silence, they were content just to be near each other. No one needed to have an answer this moment. No one needed anything this moment. They had all they needed right now.

Did I overreact? Maybe to him, this secret was the most horrific thing in his life. He had already admitted to me the game he played. And a part of me saw through it when we went to the gala. So why am I so shocked? That's why he was desperate to know what I said to those ladies – because unknowingly I was playing the game for him by just being me. He wanted to revel in it.

Charlie wasn't sure if her thoughts were making her angry or were consoling her. She was genuinely confused. What did she want? Did she want him? Or was it her pride because she felt she had been played? How bad was it what he really did? He was protecting himself from a game that other people played with him. Was there really any harm done?

"Ok, let's be done with this. I have come to the conclusion that the only reason I am angry is because I feel like you used me to get back at people at the gala. You had something to prove and you used me to prove it if that makes any sense. Truthfully, there is really no harm done except for the fact that you didn't trust my character enough within the first few weeks to know I am not like everyone else. But then a part of me says you did know that and that is why you took me to the gala. So explain yourself and tell me what you want from me." Charlie demanded.

"I really wasn't trying to prove anything. You weren't a pawn of any sorts on purpose. It does look that way and it maybe turned out that way, but it wasn't intentional. The truth is, because you had no idea who I was, I didn't have to question your motives. As I explained before, I could just be me and you could be you. I wanted to take you to the gala because I wanted to go with someone who actually wanted to be with me at the gala, not someone who wanted to go to the gala to be seen with me. Does that make any sense to you?"

"I think so – like you are some golden ticket – to be at the gala and be seen with you – the jackpot."

126

"Exactly! I'm nobody in my book but other people make me out to be someone. I don't want to ever question whether I think what someone feels for me is genuine or motivated by money or prestige or fame. If it can go as far as that," he explained

"So what do you want from me?"

"Nothing. I want you to be you."

"OK. Fair enough but I have played my part pretty cool not being the typical girl who wants to know where this is going. …but now I am ready to know where this is going. I don't want to know that you can whisk any other women away on an Italian weekend; I don't want to risk feeling like I felt when I saw you walking with your sister. So shit or get off the pot, Honey! I'm done playing it cool." By the end of her speech Charlie was yelling.

Liam was laughing, "Shit or get off the pot, Honey?

He grabbed her and started kissing her. "You belong to me. There will be no foreign excursions with other women. As I said, you don't need dance lessons because I will always be your partner. I have all I want with you. And what about you? How do you feel, Charlie?"

"Good enough. …. for now," Charlie answered.

He has all he wants in me.

They explored Taormina. They walked to churches and shopped the local stands. Lunch was delicious and fresh. The wine was amazing. Charlie couldn't help herself. She was so relaxed and happy.

"I want to live here. Forever!" turning her face up to the sun, "with you." She turned her gaze to Liam who was beaming like a proud father.

"Maybe one day, Chuck."

Liam bought two bottles of wine from the restaurant to take back to the hotel room. Dinner, she was told, was to be at an old Italian house noted for its ambiance and great food. But they still had the rest of the day to explore. So much had been explored so far, hearts, dreams, fears and wishes. And so much had been discovered.

CHAPTER 17

By the time dinner was over, it was late and the long walk back gave Charlie plenty of time to think about what was to happen next. She wanted a shower first and then she wanted a long lustful night wrapped up in Liam.

"Liam?"

"Hmm," he replied.

"That night we celebrated my raise, I woke up in your bed in your tee shirt. Did I get changed or did you help me?"

"I helped you."

"How much did you help me?" she asked seriously, dreading his answer.

"I could have put you in bed naked and you wouldn't have known the difference."

"Hmm."

"What made you think of that?"

"Not sure really. I always wanted to know but was afraid to ask."

"Why were you afraid?," he snorted

"Never mind"

"A woman's mind…. I'll never understand it"

As they entered their room, Charlie kicked off her shoes and announced she was taking a shower. After a few minutes in the bathroom with the water running, Liam came in.

"What are you doing, Liam!"

"Joining you." He lit a candle and shut the light.

Liam washed her hair and the rest of her. Charlie took her time washing every inch of his body. He was so toned and muscular. His body was absolutely perfect, more than she could say of her own. Always struggling with her body image, she knew now he had seen her completely naked and he was still here.

He has just touched every inch of you. It's time to get over it, she told herself.

He leaned his body against hers, wrapping his arms around her and resting his head on her shoulder. Charlie melted into his embrace. Both were content to feel the hot water and the tenderness of each other's touch. There was no need for conversation; so much was already being said.

Liam held Charlie as if she would disappear if he let go. His thoughts were heart wrenching. He was afraid for the first time in all his life, afraid of facing a future without her. *What would it be like to know you had held, even if it was for a small moment, the best thing ever meant for you, and you let it go?*

Charlie was relaxed, pleased to be held in the arms of the man she loved and was growing to trust. *He loves me for me.* She was beginning to believe in a real future for them. The water was getting cold but neither one noticed. The cool water was welcomed to clear their heads. Liam kissed her gently as he turned the water off. He grabbed a towel and began drying Charlie's hair, back, and legs. Never before had something so mundane been so sensual. Never before had Charlie ever felt so satisfied.

Sunday morning was bright and beautiful. They ate breakfast in the hotel while making plans for their sightseeing. It was a leisurely day with no stress. They ate gelato while walking through the area shops. Italy truly was a place for lovers.

"I really do want to stay here forever."

Liam was amazed at how well she picked up the language. She was very adaptable and wasn't shy about trying.

I love that, he thought to himself. He didn't love however how all the men looked at her when she went into the shops on her own. Italians love their woman robust. She had that dark auburn hair and brown eyes with her olive skin. She was charming and warm and the men seemed to admire her enthusiasm trying to speak their language. Not normally the jealous kind, Liam was caught off guard at his emotions.

In Edinburgh, no one would ever poach on his woman so he never had to worry. Well, almost everyone; sisters don't count.

Charlie was taking a long time in the shop so he finished his ice cream and went in after her. There were two men helping her with leather coats. She was trying them on and looking in the mirror.

"I guess I'm going to have to get a shorter one," she said out loud, knowing that neither of the men could understand a word she was saying…"To cover my butt, the top is too big."

The men looked at her. In her broken Italian she tried explaining she wanted a shorter coat. She motioned, disgusted, to her backside saying too big for a long coat.

"No, no signora, in Italy we throw away the bones," the young man responded in a thick Italian accent. Charlie laughed with a big smile to her compliment.

That was enough for Liam. "How's it going in here?"

"Fine, I always wanted a leather coat and the prices are excellent. What do you think about this one?" Charlie asked. The two men seemed disappointed at the sight of Liam. They continued to help her until she found a coat she liked.

"Excellent, I'll take this one."

Charlie was thrilled with her purchase.

"Don't you love it!" she asked Liam who was too busy making sure the men were done looking at her.

"Yes, yes, it's great."

Charlie continued to look around the shop.

"My mom would have a field day in here with all these knick knacks. She loves this stuff. Ok, I'm done. Are you?"

"Sure whenever you are ready."

Charlie walked to the front where her new coat was already packaged. Presenting her credit card, "No, no, signoro. Signoro." Charlie shook her head and kept trying to hand him her credit card.

"Signoro pagato."

"Pagato? What is pagato?"

"I already paid for it, Charlie."

She turned angry at him. "WHY?"

"I was trying to be nice."

"You already are nice. You took me on this vacation. What you are telling me is I can't shop while we are here because you will pay for it and I don't want you too." She took her package, thanked the gentleman, and walked into the blinding sunshine.

"Liam, I do have money to buy my own stuff. I am not poor and I do not expect you to buy everything, so please try to control yourself. I like to shop and I don't want to not buy something here because I'm afraid it will be awkward. Are we clear? It's hard enough for me to swallow the fact that you have paid for every ounce of this vacation, dinners, lunch. I am not a freeloader but I feel like one."

"It's your birthday present, Chuck. You can't pay for dinners and lunches."

"Well, it's not like any other birthday present I have ever had in my life. I don't expect you to be this extravagant in the future."

Liam smiled at her and she wasn't sure why. He gave her a big kiss.

"I thought British men weren't big on public displays of affection."

"Well, I guess no one ever had anyone as bewitching as you." Liam said.

The night was passionate. Neither one slept much. The reality was that they had to catch their flight by noon the next day and then it would be back to work.

They both didn't want it to end. Time after time he satisfied her and she made sure he wasn't left out.

Charlie thanked him over and over for a wonderful birthday. Wrapped in each other's arm, they watched the sun come up over the sea.

I swear I am in a movie. This is definitely a movie.

CHAPTER 18

End of December

The short, cold days of winter had Charlie longing for the summer. She was told it doesn't get dark until very late, after 11 PM at one point of the summer. She had also heard wonderful things about the Festival, the Military Tattoo, and the millions of people who flock to Edinburgh in August.

On the nights she spent with Liam, she would ask him every detail of shows he had seen over the course of his life.

"You can see whatever you want! Music, plays, skits, dramas, you name it, it's here."

He went ahead and bought two tickets to the Tattoo for one of her Christmas presents.

"So, what do you want for Christmas?" Charlie would ask him.

"Just you and a simple life" was his answer every time. Then he would continue to talk about how the streets would be filled with performers and simply walking down the High Street was fun, taking in the entire atmosphere.

Charlie was excited about the festival. She would look on the Internet sites of past years to understand what it was all about.

She thought that might be a good time for her mother to visit, since there would be so much going on. It had been nearly three months since she had arrived in Edinburgh. This would be her first Christmas spent away from her family. Her father would love it here. There were so many pictures to be taken and the history to be learned! He would have his days filled from dusk till dawn seeing it all. Nothing brought on missing family more than the holidays.

Charlie's schedule had become more routine. She had quiz night at the pub with her friend Adele when Liam worked late. On Tuesdays, she and Liam usually made dinner at his house. Depending on what the week brought, Wednesday or Thursday could see Charlie cooking a gourmet meal if their schedules allowed, otherwise going out for dinner. Weekends were for discovering Edinburgh or, if the weather was nice, Liam would take her away overnight to a charming village nestled in the heartland.

The office was producing more than ever and staff retention was no longer a problem. Once bonus checks started rolling out, she thought the team would follow her into battle if she asked. Louise had filled Ann's position perfectly and was becoming a friend as well. They would go shopping or get their nails done occasionally. Work seemed to be going fine and Charlie was pleased, although there was still no replacement for Mr. Duval's position.

"Liam, please, tell me what you want for Christmas," Charlie begged.
"I told you, you and a simple life."
"But you have me and I need to put something underneath that tree!!"
"You'll have to come up with something on your own then."
Charlie had spent the last week racking her brain over what to get him. There were the cliché gifts like a tie, slippers, or a dress shirt but she really wanted something a little more personal. She had thought about getting him a massage but Louise had told her there were a lot of insalubrious places with bad reputations. She con-

sidered an expensive bottle of champagne but it seemed too vague. Christmas was four days away and she was no closer to a solution.

Walking home from the quiz, Charlie thought of the perfect gift. A humidor filled with excellent cigars for all the nights he worked late. She also decided to get him a bottle of designer cologne she found when shopping with Adele.

Charlie felt very relieved to have finally come up with an idea.

She was climbing the steps to her apartment, thinking of asking Louise tomorrow where she could get a humidor, when she was stopped dead in her tracks. Her heart started beating in terror. She squinted her eyes to make sure what she was seeing was accurate. Her apartment door was open. She backed away slowly, never turning her back on the door. She reached for her cell phone as she carefully took one step at a time until she could make a run for it out the street level door.

She dialed 999 as the door closed behind her. She started running back to the pub. She was giving the police all the details when she reached the entrance to the pub. Charlie remained outside with a view of her street level door to see if anyone strange came out.

The next call was to Liam. Terrified, she panted "Lee, someone's broke into my apartment. I called the police."

He could hear the fear in her shaking voice.

"Where are you?"

"I ran back to the pub but I am outside watching my door. The police are on their way."

"So am I. Stay there until the police arrive at your place. When they do, do not go up with them until they have been in there first. I'll be there in two minutes. Stay put!"

Charlie waited. It felt like forever but she heard the sirens on their way and prayed Liam would get there first. She felt sick.

Who would want to break into my apartment? How did they get in the stair door? My neighbors had to have heard something. Why would someone do this?

Liam drove up and Charlie got in his car.

"Are you OK?," he asked, concerned.

"Not really. Why would someone want to break into my apartment? Do you think it's because they know I am hardly there? But if they are watching my comings and goings they would know that tonight I always stay there."

Her stream of thoughts was pouring out as Liam parked in front of her place and got out. The police were there. Charlie sat in the car. Liam spoke with a few of the officers. They all were looking up as if they could see her flat from the street.

After a few minutes, Liam came over, "They are going to need you to go up and see what's missing. They have checked the place out and no one is in there. They are currently speaking to your neighbors."

Opening the car door for her, Liam grabbed her hand and escorted her upstairs. "It's all right, Chuck. I'm coming with you. You can stop shaking. I promise it's going to be all right."

At the top of her steps, an officer was chatting with one of her neighbors and the other neighbor was standing in the hall.

"I'm so sorry for all the interruption tonight." Charlie offered. Mr. Simmons nodded. Charlie walked into her apartment.

"Oh my God! They have destroyed my apartment! Look, they broke everything they possibly could."

Walking quickly through each room, taking in all the devastation, Charlie felt violated. She leaned against the wall. She covered her face with her hands and pressed her fingertips into her temples.

"I can't believe this has happened," she said, overcome, "I can't believe it."

"Ma'am, if you can, look about and see if you notice anything missing; we would appreciate it. I understand this is difficult. A crew will be here shortly for fingerprints. Do you have somewhere to stay tonight or should we call a locksmith?"

"She'll be staying with me," Liam answered.

"Thank you, Mr. Marshall. If you could help the lady check through the flat that would be great."

Liam took Charlie's hand and began asking her questions about what someone would have wanted or been looking for. Charlie had no idea and thought it was perhaps a random act.

"I'm glad I left my laptop at the office or I'm sure that would have been taken. Nothing really seems to be gone, although I'm not sure why they rummaged through my food. I'm going to have to throw everything out! I'm afraid they did something to it!"

"Nothing is missing?," Liam asked, shocked.

"Nothing that is sticking out to me right now. I really don't have much here, nothing of value anyway. I don't even have a TV."

The officer's were making their reports and more personnel arrived. Pictures were taken, then fingerprints and statements. Liam got out a suitcase and told her to pack her stuff. Charlie did as she was told.

"I can't imagine why with all the apartments in Edinburgh, they would pick mine. Odds like that don't exist. Why wouldn't they pick something off the main street? Why wouldn't they wait until the middle of the night?"

Charlie had been home after work to change and didn't leave to go to the quiz until 7:30 PM.

138

Who ever did this was in and out between 7:30 and 11PM, hardly a usual time to rob someone.
It was starting to feel like it wasn't a random act.

By 12:30 AM, they were at Liam's house.
"Can I call Mr. Moore and tell him what happened?," she asked, not wanting to take advantage.
"You don't have to ask to use the phone, Charles."
Charlie called Mr. Moore and explained what had happened. He seemed moderately concerned. Charlie advised him she would be taking some time off in the morning to get new locks fitted and her place cleaned up. With that out of the way, she poured herself a glass of wine.

"Liam, what are you doing tomorrow?" she asked bashfully. He turned to look at her. "I'm afraid to be there now and I have to clean up," she said with a cheesy grin.
"You can come with me to the office tomorrow. I'll only be there for a minute or two and then we can head over to your flat. OK?"
He was a wonderful man.
"Thanks. Did I tell you lately that I love you?"
"Actually, no, you haven't" he teased.
Charlie grabbed him and kissed him, "Well, I do."
"Don't forget that" was his simple answer.

CHAPTER 19

Christmas morning started out with a passionate present in bed.

"You're going to kill this old man, Charlie" Liam teased, out of breath.

"So sorry. I'll never let it happen again. Merry Christmas."

"Merry Christmas, my love."

"I'll go put the coffee on, you rest and regain your strength. I know I can be so demanding, especially on someone your age."

Charlie laughed as she put on Liam's robe and his slippers. "Gonna borrow these. Hope you don't mind," she said sarcastically.

The coffee was brewing when the phone rang. Liam answered and Charlie assumed it was his family. They were all getting together tomorrow, Boxing Day, instead of Christmas, so the men could watch soccer - or football - as she had been corrected many times. This would be her first time to actually meet his sister Jessica face to face since she saw them on the street that horrible day. This would also be her first time meeting Liam's father.

Charlie was very nervous about the whole day to come.

"Charlie, pick up the phone, Mother wants to wish you a merry Christmas," Liam yelled down.

"Hello, Mrs. Marshall. Merry Christmas" Charlie and Charlotte spoke without difficulty for the next ten minutes. She knew all about her break-in and was sympathetic to her being away from home for the holidays.

The phone call did calm Charlie's nerves some but she still was not looking forward to facing Jessica.

Charlie brought Liam's coffee up and urged him to get out of bed, "I'm excited for you to open your presents!! Come on, hurry up!" Liam laughed at her childlike spirit and obliged her.

"Well now that I have caught my breath, I guess I could make it down the steps...unless you want to have a double feature? I'm always up for a replay"

"Liam! Please!"

Heading back downstairs, Charlie retrieved Liam's gifts from 'the dark room' as it had come to be called, and placed them under the tree.

"All that's for me?" he asked.

"Shut up, stop it." Charlie demanded, embarrassed.

When Liam placed himself on the couch, she handed him the big box.

"This one first. I really didn't know what to get you and this was the best thing I thought of. I hope you like it."

Liam was enchanted by how excited Charlie was. She loved Christmas and it must be hard for her to be away from her family.

"Excellent! I have been meaning to buy one of these. Well done. I love it," he commented on seeing the handsome humidor.

"Open it up, go ahead, open it!"

Liam opened the humidor to find it packed with all sorts of expensive cigars. He read each label.

"You must have done your homework to pick out such fine cigars. Charlie, some of these are quite expensive, what are you buying them for? I don't want you to spend your money on me."

Looking at her face, he realized she took great pleasure in presenting the gift to him and he wasn't being a good recipient.

"I'm sorry, Charles. The cigars are world class. Splendid gift. Thank you."

"Do you really like it?"

"I love it, honestly. There are enough cigars in here to last me the whole New Year."

"Great! And there's more, just a few small things."

Liam unwrapped his new cologne and Charlie had stuffed a stocking with candy and silly things.

"Charles, thank you so much. This was wonderful. I especially liked my stocking. I can't tell you the last time I ate a lollipop. Now, your turn."

Liam grabbed one of the two boxes under the tree and handed it to her. She was radiantly flushed with excitement.

"Ooh, I love Christmas." She unwrapped an elegant robe. It was sinfully soft.

"I guess you're sick of me stealing yours."

"Yes, this one stays here," he directed.

The second box had a pair of slippers.

"Same premise, I suppose? These stay here too?" she asked guiltily.

"You got it!"

"Well thank you, Liam, all very appropriate and I love them."

She got off the couch and gave him a big kiss.

"And there's more!" he teased.

"More? No Liam that's enough really."

"Be a gracious recipient." Liam went to a closet in which Charlie had never been. He grabbed a few bags, all filled with wrapped presents.

"You are kidding, right? Those are for your family tomorrow, right?"

"No, they are all for you!"

Charlie felt a little uncomfortable at how many gifts there were. "This isn't right Liam, that's too much. The robe and slippers were great and fitting. This is over-kill."

"Wheesht, and open them."

One by one Charlie went through the gifts. There was a hair dryer, a tooth brush, pajamas, socks, gift certificates to clothing stores and shoe stores, nail stuff, more hair stuff, her favorite face cream. You name it that she used, he had it.

"Liam, this is ridiculous!"

"No it's not. I figured since I asked you to start keeping some of your belongings here and you didn't, then I would buy you some necessities to keep here. So all of this stays here, including whatever you buy with the gift certificates."

Charlie was stunned and speechless. "Ally is never ever going to believe this. I told her before but this is the top. You are some man, Liam."

"Just remember that," he grinned.

They settled in by the fire. They had a late break-fast and later in the afternoon, Charlie phoned a few of her friends and then home. She was wrapped in her new robe.

Charlie couldn't remember a time when she felt more together. She had a great career going, a man that seemed to cherish her, and she was comfortable with it all. There was no overwhelming drama other than the break-in.

"Charlie? Can you come upstairs for a second?" Liam yelled. Charlie went up to his bedroom.

"OK. So here are two drawers for you. I have cleared a space in the closet for your new clothes and a shoe rack for your shoes."

Liam walked into the bathroom. "Here is a drawer and cabinet for you as well. If you need more space, then we'll talk, perhaps work it out in trade," he joked.

Charlie had known many defining moments in her life. She was, however, not prepared for this one. She thought the clothes and so forth would be kept in the other bedroom. Even though, since their return from Italy, she had been sleeping in Liam's room, she never imagined he would want her stuff there when there was another whole closet sitting empty. It seemed... permanent...committed.

"Wow, you really caught me off guard with this one, Liam," Charlie said, sounding cautious. "You're making me feel like I'm moving in."

"I wouldn't say moving in. I would say we are making things more convenient for us. I argue my case again that every morning you stay here we have to go by your flat to get something. This way, we can finish our cup of coffee together before going. Let's be honest, you do your wash here and, one night maybe two, you spend at your flat."

He's a good man, she told herself. *You should be jumping up and down for joy.*

"Right." She answered. Now she had drama. Charlie was unsure why she hesitated. Perhaps a few of her own fears or insecurities had surfaced for a moment, she decided. She was definitely caught off guard by Liam's seemingly effortless step forward in their relationship. It was a step she never considered herself. But now, it was done.

CHAPTER 20

Boxing day. The ride to Livingston wasn't too long. In fact, it went too fast for Charlie and her nerves. She was going to have to meet Jessica. She did not ask if Rebekah was going to be there, although she highly doubted it. Charlie had no wishes to see what Liam's ex-fiancée looked like anyway. The phantom standard that she felt she had to live up to was enormous enough without seeing it live and exclusive. Judging by Rebekah's looks, the ex, she was sure, wasn't some Jerry Springer, Twinkie-eating, trailer-park redneck.

"Are you sure I look OK?" Charlie asked, needing a bit of extra reassurance.

"You look gorgeous! As you always do," Liam answered sincerely.

"And you are sure the gifts we got for your family are OK? And we didn't need to bring any food other than the wine?"

"You are fine, Loops, honestly, I wouldn't steer you wrong. Jessica knows what went on. She completely understood your reaction. She said in your place, she would have walked right up and started punching the other woman. So she was thrilled you just went away. She said she doesn't look good in black and blue." The small jest did make Charlie chuckle.

The house was gorgeous and huge, even by American standards. It was all brick and set in a rural community of about six houses. Each house had to be on at least two acres. Some had horses and other animals. It was beautiful.

"Mother, Merry Christmas." Liam greeted the family and introduced Charlie to everyone - Jessica's husband, Rob, Liam's father, Duncan, and a few aunts and uncles. Charlie was trying to figure out who was the direct descendant of the Queen but wasn't sure whose side of the family the aunts and uncles were from - his father or mother. Everyone was very polite and welcoming.

"Hello, Jessica. It's nice to finally meet you under more proper circumstances," Charlie offered. *Get it over with.*

"Yes, I agree. It is nice to finally meet someone who can keep my brother in line."

"I think he keeps *me* in line."

The girls laughed and the awkwardness subsided in minutes. Charlie liked Jessica. She was a real, down to earth lady. Rob was the same. He was wearing blue jeans with a sport coat. He was comfortable with the family, Charlie could tell, even though she came decked out with the black pants suit and pearls.

Wine was poured and the conversations ranged from sports and politics to food and weather. The fire was crackling and the house smelled wonderful.

"So, Charlie," Duncan asked, "How do you love our Edinburgh?"

Charlie went on about how much Liam had shown her and how the scope of the age of everything was finally starting to sink in. She spoke of her excitement for the Festival and how she wanted her family to come visit.

Before long, dinner was ready and everyone was seated at the table. She talked with everyone and no one gave the impression of having to endure her, so all in all, she thought she was doing a pretty good job at presenting herself. Short of anything horrible going wrong like backing up the toilet or letting out a belch, she was home free. Liam had left her alone to fend for herself

146

before dinner. Seated next to each other now, he gave her hand a quick squeeze. The table looked fit for a magazine cover. Dinner was delicious and perfect.

With everyone's bellies full, Charlie wondered if this would be like Thanksgiving back home when the men would instinctively unbutton their pants and fall asleep watching football, but somehow she felt this wasn't that type of family. What a laugh Liam would have at the informality of her family rituals. It wasn't uncommon for Christmas day to be spent in sweatpants in preparation for the copious amounts of food being cooked. There would be kids running all around, several TV's on, and there was always someone who was sick. Chaotic and loud came to mind - a sharp contrast to the meal that was just served with classical music playing gently in the background.

Everyone had moved back into the living room. Liam, his father, and Rob lit cigars.

"Father, for my Christmas, Charlie presented me with the most handsome humidor filled with exquisite cigars from all over. I brought these couple …"

Duncan immediately looked at each cigar, praising her choices.

"Excellent choice, young lady, however did you know which ones to pick?" he inquired.

"Well, I did some research about what makes a good cigar. Then I went down to one of the better tobacconists and asked a lot of questions. They were very helpful."

"And what did Liam get you for your Christmas?" Charlie was horrified. *How in the hell do I answer that? Um, your son bought me a wardrobe of clothes so I can shack up with him basically since I spend the night there so much. Don't think that will go over well.*

Charlie glanced at Liam, panicked. He answered smoothly, "Actually father, I have not given Charlie her present yet."

Charlie raised her eyebrows at him in question.

"I was waiting until after dinner." Liam reached into his pocket and pulled out a beautifully wrapped box. Charlie's heart was pounding.

Does it get any more embarrassing than this? Now I have to open this gift in front of everyone and it's obviously jewelry. Everything was going so well.

"That's for me?" she asked surprised.

"Yes, that's for you."

"Well, shouldn't everyone open their gifts then? I'm a bit embarrassed," Charlie stated shyly.

"All right then, everyone grab a present," Liam ordered. With everyone scurrying about to find gifts with their name on it, Charlie shot Liam a look. She meant this look this time. It was the 'what the hell are you trying to do to me?' look followed by the 'you shouldn't be buying me stuff like this' look. She thought he got the message.

Charlie took the brief moment of confusion to open the box. The maroon velvet box lifted open to reveal a gorgeous pair of pearl earrings.

"Liam, they are beautiful. Thank you so much."

"I decided since your grandmother bought you the necklace in Italy, then I would buy you the earrings in Italy."

"You bought these on our trip?"

"Yes."

Charlie was flabbergasted at how thoughtful and sentimental he was.

"Well, I love them." She got up to give him a hug and a kiss. "Thank you, they are stunning," Charlie said as she put them on.

With all the presents being opened, Charlie watched. Again differences between the two families arose in her mind. Her dad's gifts ranged from exquisitely framed personal pictures taken during the year to more safety conscious/practical items like windshield washer fluid and batteries. Her mother always gave an article or two of clothing or the knickknacks that Charlie despised because they would only be needing to be dusted in a few days.

The gifts here were expensive jewelry and imported bottles of champagne, French clothing and Italian designed suits – high-ticket items. Everything was very formal.

"This one is for you, Darling," chimed Charlotte.

"Mrs. Marshall, that wasn't necessary, truly," Charlie commented.

"I know, Dear, but that is what makes Christmas so much fun, none of it is ever necessary, and for those of us who love to shop, well then, it's just an excuse to spend. I hope you enjoy it," she said lovingly.

Charlie unwrapped an elegant scarf. The lush burgundy and black velvet was mixed with a sheer cream silk.

"Charlotte, this is amazing! With a crisp starched white blouse, I will look like a million dollars. Thank you so much. And the sash you are wearing is beautiful as well." Charlie's reaction must have been exactly what Charlotte was looking for because she smiled from ear to car.

"I'm so glad you like it, wear it in good health. This is our Marshall tartan." Charlotte said holding the sash in her hands delicately. "I find it to be one of the most attractive of plaids with the combination of blue and green mixing flawlessly"

Charlie smiled back and realized she had called her Charlotte. Charlie had not asked Liam how he wished her to address his parents since they seemed to be so formal. No notice was paid so she thought she got away with it.

As everyone hugged and kissed good-bye, Charlie realized she had really had a good time.

"Liam, that was a very nice time. I hope I didn't embarrass you in anyway."

"Don't be daft, Chuck."

During the ride home, they chatted about New Years Eve. The Hogmanay Celebration in Scotland is world famous and not even New York compares.

"I'm not really a New Year's Eve chick, Liam. I have never had a good New Year's Eve. It always seems to be a let down. The past few years, I have actually stayed home reflecting on the past and dreaming of the future," she said.

"Well, this year you are going out. You will be accompanying me to a very prestigious affair in the north. We will leave the day before New Year's Eve."

"Liam, my love," Charlie said sarcastically, "You do realize, yet again, these types of things you must tell me about or we will continue to run into dress situations like we did a few months back. Again, I do not have clothes to wear to a party of that magnitude and from what you are telling me, this is a few day event in which case I do not have clothes full stop to even sit in the company of such people."

"I sorted it for you. The ladies at the shop always keep a file on each customer, so I stopped in a few weeks ago and they have prepared a wardrobe for you for the whole three days," Liam said, very proud of himself.

"I'm not sure if I'm angry or relieved but really you have to stop dressing me."

"You said in Italy that these types of events aren't your thing. You don't like them or the people. So I figured that if I made it as simple as possible for you then you would continue to go with me because I have to go

150

to these events. You being there makes me happy." Liam's statement was more of a confession than anything.

"I see. How do you know the clothes will fit?"

"You have a fitting tomorrow after work. She assured me they would have everything ready the next evening with whatever alterations are necessary."

"Shoes?" she reminded him.

"Covered" he answered.

"Accessories?" she asked.

"Eight completed ensembles was my request."

The jousting ended with Charlie snorting, "I don't have work tomorrow, by the way. Mr. Moore told me not to return till after the New Year. It was my gift from him for covering Mr. Duval's spot so long and so well."

"And when were you going to tell me that?" he asked shocked.

"I guess right now considering you work on Mondays and I normally do too. So tonight, I guess I have to go back to my scary apartment," Charlie declared with a bit of disgust for her situation.

"In your mind, Charles, because I am not home you think you can't be at my place?"

"I realize this is a trick question, therefore I plead the 5th on the grounds that I may incriminate myself. Although I am sure it is no secret I am chicken to stay at my apartment alone at the best of times, let alone now that someone has violated me."

"I'll have my secretary run a key over to you in the morning so you can come and go as you like."

"You have a secretary? And she has a key to your house?! Why does your secretary have a key to your house?" Charlie was getting loud and angry.

"Hold on! I didn't say she had one. I said she would run one over, meaning after I get one made in the morning. Really, Chuck, we have to work on this jealousy thing," Liam affirmed while shaking his head.

"It's not so much a jealousy thing as it is 'I don't know who the players are in the game.' I had no idea you had a secretary. How old is she?"

Liam burst out in laughter. "Honestly, I have no idea. She looks to be about 20. I hired her because of her luscious locks of blonde hair and her tight skirts. I love how she brings me my coffee each morning with my messages smelling of her perfume. She also works late with me on Monday nights." Liam wished he could see Charlie's expressions.

"That's enough," Charlie said laughing along with him, knowing he was teasing her.

"Mrs. Niddrie is probably as old as ages with Moses at this point. If you wish to learn how to tie your hair in a bun so tight that it's actually an alternative to a face lift then she is your woman."

"Good," was Charlie's satisfied answer.

"Charlie?"

"Yeah"

"This Hogmanay Party is the one that will start the tabloids."

"Great," Charlie said with a big sigh, "remind me not to pick my nose and to check my shoes for toilet paper. I really do not want to go"

"I know."

CHAPTER 21

Charlie slept late and when she awoke Liam was already gone. She pulled out her laptop and started in on a bit of work. The end of the month and the end of the year had tons of reports that went along with them. The conversion in October to combine all the data and get everyone on uniform software left a lot of holes. Charlie had been manually going through each missing or improperly coded transaction so the year-end reports would be accurate. However, there were so many inconsistencies in transactions, she wasn't sure how the reports would look. More than a few unexplainable transactions had occurred and the record keeping for those was shoddy. Charlie wasn't familiar with the tax system and it was all under the tax codes that these transactions had taken place. She would have to do some more research.

She spoke with Louise and got her messages. She liked working from home, even if it wasn't her home. By the afternoon, showered and ready to go, her key hadn't yet arrived.

"Liam," she said, as he answered his cell phone.

"Hi, Dear, sleep well?"

"Yes, thanks. I was going to head out and run a few errands then hit my appointment for my clothes. Tell *your secretary* there is no need for the key."

"She isn't there yet? She left ages ago. Hmmm," Liam said thoughtfully, "No bother, I'll call her. Have fun and I hope you like what they picked out for you. Oh, what's for dinner?"

"Wow, nothing makes a woman feel more like a wife then 'What's for dinner?'" Charlie laughed, "I'll pick up some groceries on the way back to your house and whip you up something stupendous."

"A wife…didn't think you'd go down that road. Call me and I'll pick you up because you may be able to take some of the clothes home with you."

"Ok, but I don't want to stop at my house so I'll still bring them to your house," she answered quickly.

"That's what I meant," he answered.

"Oh."

Home. He's calling his house my home. He wants me to keep my stuff there. I thought it was the women who were always three steps ahead of the men.

The clothes were unreal. So classy she felt like a fraud wearing them. Each ensemble had a matching bag, shoes or boots and jewelry. Whether the jewelry was real or not, she had no idea, and she wasn't about to ask. This must have all cost him thousands. Each piece fit impeccably, not one ounce of tailoring was required.

Pulling out her credit card she proceeded to the front while everything was packaged.

"Thank you all so much. Everything is beautiful," Charlie said handing the lady her credit card.

"Sir Liam has already taken care of the charges," the no-name lady announced.

"I see. Does he require a copy of the bill?"

"It will be mailed to him."

"OK, well then thanks again for everything. I'm going to wait a few minutes for Liam to pick me up."

Charlie called Liam and he said he would be there shortly. While Charlie waited, she looked through the clothes. The prices were ridiculous. *How does he make enough money to pay for all of this? He really only works on Mondays.*

"So, Sir Liam tells us you are going up north for your Hogmanay celebration. We outfitted a few ladies for that soiree. It will be a grand affair. I would love to go myself."

154

"Yes, Liam says it's very nice. I am excited to see that part of the country."

"These types of affairs must be quite different than what you're used to." The old codger turned up her nose.

"Actually no," Charlie said with the same air of confidence, "I am used to senators and presidents, nearly the same as your upper echelons here. Only they work."

The lady grimaced, "I meant no offense."

"I'm sure you never do." Charlie shot back. Liam arrived and Charlie jumped in.

The next few days that led up to the New Year's party were quiet and relaxed. They spent a lot of time together and Charlie played the role of housewife well. She worked more on the conversion errors and asked Liam about the tax codes. He looked over a few things with her and helped as best he could.

Nights were steamy and mornings were no longer awkward. Charlie felt comfortable in their relationship, especially since it had been discussed so openly in Italy.

He had given her a key to his place and he had kept the key to hers. His secretary would call and speak to her on a first name basis, as would his mother. Charlie had a boyfriend.

"Are you ready?" he asked impatiently.

"Yes, yes. I think I have everything," Charlie answered hurriedly.

"Do you have everything?" she asked back at him.

"I got you, that's all I need," he joked.

The car ride up north was very hairy. It was sleeting and the roads were narrow and unlit. Liam seemed to know the road well enough but Charlie was wishing they would arrive soon because she was scared. Not wanting to even go, she thought it was ironic that arriving would be a relief.

"So, are these going to be the same people as the gala?" she asked tentatively.

"You'll see a few familiar faces."

"Will I be cornered in the bathroom again?" she reminded him of before.

"Probably."

"Great," the sarcasm was evident.

One of the things Charlie didn't have was a proper coat. It was very cold and damp. As they hurried into the castle, Charlie was not prepared for the onslaught of people so soon. Everyone was in the reception area, greeting them and taking note of her. She noticed their faces saying *Her again?*

Why did I agree to come to this?

Their room was cozy. It had a fireplace and en suite bathroom. There was an itinerary on the small table. Charlie picked it up and read it over it. There were luncheons, Bridge games, whisky and wine tastings, whist, high teas, and the list went on. It seemed more like camp for rich people than a celebration. The evenings had formal affairs, live entertainment, and six-course dinners.

"We certainly won't be bored," Charlie commented. Liam was unpacking his things and Charlie followed suit.

"You brought a kilt?" she was shocked.

"Yes, all self-respecting Scotsmen wear a kilt on Hogmanay."

"I have yet to see you in a kilt. Now I'm excited. I hope I can control myself."

"Do try," he said with a wink.

So the evening was set. They were to get changed and join the rest of the participants at 5PM for drinks in Simpson Hall, to be followed by dinner and dancing.

"See, Liam. I knew I should have taken dance lessons. What do I do if someone asks me to dance?" she worried.

"No one will ask you to dance."

"Why not? I think I'm offended now!"

"You can't have it both ways. So which way do you want?" he asked confused.

"Well, I don't want to dance with someone else but I do want people to want to dance with me. I think that's it." She was laughing at how absurd she sounded.

"Chuck, really. This isn't a school Qually."

"What's that?"

"It's the first real dance you go to in school. I think you are perhaps around 11 or 12 when you go."

"I'm nervous."

"Pull yourself together," Liam said, for the first time sounding nervous himself.

Perhaps I should keep my thoughts to myself.

She donned her first outfit. She looked amazing, Liam commented. They arrived a few minutes late. Liam handed her a glass of champagne, "Pace yourself, you didn't get another raise."

Charlie snickered. She was introduced to too many people. There were photographers snapping pictures of everyone mingling. *He said this was going to be a tabloid event.* Liam never left her side. She was quite thankful. Dinner was long. It lasted over two hours. Several ladies came over and made cheap shots at her. They didn't get by Liam. Charlie made sure she kept a smile on her face. After midnight they excused themselves.

Although the ladies comments kept repeating in her head, she didn't speak of it. Liam wanted her here so that's all that mattered. To be on the safe side, Charlie reminded Liam of those special qualities that she did possess as she made him shudder and moan with pleasure several times.

"Not bad for an old man," she teased. He was already sleeping. Charlie wasn't tired. She lay in the bed, not able to shut off her mind. *Why would he subject himself to such harsh criticism and keep bringing me to such things? He realizes it. He has to. I do love him. He never said it straightforward like I did in Italy. Hmmm?*

Charlie got up and put on a pair of jeans. Bundled up, she went for a walk by the loch. It was very cold. The crisp air was invigorating however. Her thoughts ran away with her and she pictured Liam involved in all sorts of charades. Then she remembered Ally's words – "Perhaps he really does like you for you." *A bit far fetched,* Charlie thought, *but possibly.* The sound of the water lapping on the rocks by the shoreline was very soothing. She felt more at peace and headed back to the room.

Liam was still sleeping, completely unaware that she had even gone. She crawled back into bed and snuggled in.

"Where'd you go?" a sleepy voice came.

"I'm sorry, did I wake you?" she asked.

"I woke up and you weren't here."

"I went for a walk by the loch."

"Any particular reason?" he inquired.

"I was trying to sort out why you would bring me to these things, knowing people are going to talk about you bringing someone not..." *Oh boy, Charlie, now you've backed yourself into another corner.* She struggled to finish, "someone not in the social scenes these folks seem to be in."

"Charlie, I don't need the approval of these people on anything I do. I have not come to this party for two

158

years. I love it up here and was pleased to have someone I loved to come with me."

"Oh so you brought your fiancée with you before to this party?"

"Well, of course."

"Oh." Small word but it spoke volumes.

"Look, whatever your issue is, please move beyond it." That was an order.

The next day saw Liam and Charlie separated for different activities. She went to play bridge with the ladies and the men went to play whist. Charlie got the feeling that this was the sort of thing that people did in the olden days. Liam gave her a quick kiss and a small pep talk about how she would be fine.

This is going to be a nightmare. She sat at a table for four. The game began and thanks to the time she had wasted in college playing computer games, she had learned how to play. For the first half hour, all present minded their manners, but suddenly, like a switch had been flipped, all gloves came off.

"So, Charlie, how are finding the good life?" one bitch started.

"I beg your pardon?" Charlie snapped.

"Well, we all know, I mean it's no secret, that you are, shall we say, blue collar. Liam was never one for following the rules."

"I'm so sorry for you that you feel the need to try to demean me. I do not see any wedding rings on your finger, shall we focus on why?" Charlie was spitting mad. "Perhaps you should do some research before you start casting aspersions."

"Are you trying to insinuate that you are of wealth and class?"

"No, I am saying you shouldn't assume that is all a woman wants in her life. It may be all you want, but I, on the other hand require more than volunteer work. My happiness is something you wouldn't understand. I am goal driven. There is no secret about what drives you."

The woman pinched her lips. No one else said a word.

This sucks. Thanks Liam. After the game was finished, every one changed tables. Charlie excused herself. She listened for a moment outside the room. The chatter started with giggles and snickers.

Charlie changed back into civilian clothes and went for her walk. She too liked it up here. She just wished she didn't have to be here with these malicious, spiteful people. Lunch was probably being served and Liam would be worried sick. If she stayed gone, people would probably talk more. *Who cares! Let them talk.*

The sky was gray and the clouds looked ready to burst. It was still very cold. That didn't matter; it was just as cold inside. Charlie watched the gulls fly and dive in the loch for fish. She skipped a few stones on the water and watched a fisherman bring in his nets. His dog barked at the birds as the man yelled at the dog for scaring the fish. The wind started up making the loch ripple and the raindrops soon started.

I had better head back. Getting to her feet, she took a deep breath for courage. She turned to leave as the storm started to unleash its fury. She picked up her pace. The wind was whipping and making her way up the hill became incredibly difficult. The rain stung as it hit her face. She lowered her head to escape the pain. The dog started barking again. She glanced over her shoulder to see the boat tipping over. The dog was in the water and there was no sign of the fisherman. Charlie stood fighting the wind and rain, waiting for the man to surface. *It's too long. It's too long. He should be up by now.* She started to run toward the water, holding her hands in front of her face as a shield. The dog was swimming to shore.

"Sir? Sir!!" she was yelling breathless. Perhaps he was stuck under the boat. Charlie had no idea how deep the loch was but she ran straight into it. She swam as fast as she could over to the boat, the wind and rain working against her. It seemed like it took forever for her to reach the boat. She flipped the boat over. The fisherman was not there. She took a huge breath and dove down as deep as she could. Nothing. She did it again and then again, this time thinking she felt something.

One more time, Charlie, one more time. She was freezing. The water was frigid. Her teeth were chattering uncontrollably. She dove down and snatched with her hands at whatever it was that was there. She had grabbed the man's jacket. *This is heavy.* She struggled with it.

She surfaced and realized that the man was still in his jacket. She straightened him so his face was not in the water. Charlie floated on her back as she placed the man face up on her stomach and she did the backstroke as best she could toward shore. She could hardly breathe. The cold sucked the air out of her lungs. Her arms burned. She kicked her feet fast and hard but the shoreline still seemed miles away.

Hold on, please, hold on, we are almost there. Hold on. There was no feeling left in her legs and her arms screamed with pain. Charlie dragged his body on shore and started CPR. She wasn't really sure how to do it, but she tried. *Please, sir, please!! BREATHE!! Breathe, damn it, breathe!* He had been under the water for at least two minutes. Someone from the castle must have seen what was going on because people started running toward the loch. Liam was the first one.

"Breathe! 1,2,3,4,5" she counted as she pumped the man's chest. The dog was circling, barking. Liam dropped to his knees and waited for her to finish her mouth-to-mouth, then he pumped the fisherman's chest,

161

"1,2,3,4,5, GO!" They repeated this several more times until finally the man started coughing and spewing up water.

People running from the castle brought blankets and wrapped them around Charlie and the fisherman. He was still unconscious. The ambulance was on its way but they were so secluded it would take a while for it to arrive. They had to get the man into the warmth of the castle. Four men undertook to carry him, as Charlie followed close behind.

Once inside, they used more blankets, hot water bottles, any thing they could to warm up the fisherman. A gentleman amongst the guests was a doctor. He began checking the vital signs and barking out orders to stabilize the man.

The dog! Charlie dropped her blanket and ran back outside to find the dog. He was waiting not far from the door.

"Come here, Buddy. You have got to be cold too. Come on, come with me." Charlie brought the wet dog up to her room. No one noticed since everyone was attending to the fisherman.

Charlie's lips were blue and her teeth were still chattering. She ran the shower and put the dog in the bathroom with her in hopes the steam would warm him.

At first, the hot water felt like needles hitting her skin but soon she was warm. After drying off, she dried the dog with the towels. She attempted the blow dryer but he wasn't having much of that. He seemed all right. He wasn't shivering. She was pretty confident he would be OK. Charlie dressed and before she left to go down stairs, she filled a bowl of water for the dog.

"Liam!" she said urgently as she saw him in the hall outside their room.

"Charlie!" he hugged her and kissed her. "Are you OK?" His words were filled with worry.

"I'm fine. How is the fisherman?"

"The doc says he's not too bad vital sign wise but they don't know how his brain will be. He said sometimes when people are underwater too long, things don't always repair properly."

"Oh no. I have the dog in our room. I tried to blow him dry. He didn't like it. We may need to get him some food."

Liam was looking at her. "You saved a man's life, Charlie. You risked your own life to do it. You could have gone into shock with the temperature of that water."

"So, are you mad or proud? I can't tell?" she questioned.

"I couldn't be more proud of anyone. You are one hell of a woman." He beamed.

They went downstairs and checked on the fisherman. The ambulance was there, preparing him for departure. Charlie wanted something hot to eat and sat in front of the fire with a cup of tea while Liam did her bidding and went to make arrangements.

The ladies from the game were also in the room. No one approached her. She was fine with that.

I did save a man's life. I can't believe I just saved a man's life.

The reality of what she had done began to sink in. She felt like she was going to cry but knew she couldn't. The men now came into the room. The doctor came over, "You saved his life, Ms. Watson. Thanks to you, someone's wife is getting a different kind of phone call than the one she could have been receiving. You acted with bravery and courage. I'm not sure how many people would have done what you just did." He extended his hand. Charlie stood up and firmly shook the doctor's hand.

"Thank you, Sir," she acknowledged with a tear in her eye. "I hope he is OK."

"Well, at least he has a chance now." As the doctor walked away, everyone was looking at her. She sat back down and watched the fire. Liam pulled up a chair next to her.

"He is a very nice man," Charlie said glancing over to the doctor.

"He is the Government Chief Medical Officer."

"What does that mean?"

"He is equivelent to your US Surgeon General. He is an esteemed man."

Charlie took it easy the rest of the day. It was New Year's Eve and she wanted to save her strength for tonight. She debated on whether or not to tell Liam about the ladies this afternoon. She decided not to. Liam made sure the dog was fed and walked. The hospital called and the fisherman, whose name turned out to be Dougal Macpherson, was going to be OK. His wife was greatly thankful and their son would be by shortly to collect the dog.

"I like that dog," Charlie said, sad to see him leave. His named turned out to be Beacon, which fit the golden lab.

Liam was dressed in his kilt. Charlie wanted him right then and there when she saw him. The bright green and blue plaid of the Marshall tartan was gorgeous on Liam. It was the same colors as the sash Charlotte had worn on Boxing Day. Her own gown matched perfectly to the shade of blue in Liam's kilt. The party was excellent. The champagne was flowing as they watched groups of four enjoy performing the Highland Reel. The piper changed the tempo and everyone joined in for

Scottish country dancing. As the clock ticked closer to midnight, the group assembled in the middle of the hall. The countdown ended with bells ringing, cheers and horns, and a kiss from Liam that made her melt.

This is going to be a good year.

The drones from the bagpipes started up, gaining everyone's attention. A circle was formed as Auld Lang Syne began to play. Each person crossed their arms in front of their chests to hold the hands of their neighbors as they sang. The circle swayed back and forth until the song ended. Empty glasses were quickly refilled.

Charlie and Liam danced and talked with so many nice people that Charlie forgot all about the ones from earlier. She had a great time. So did Liam.

Floating down the hallway toward their room, Charlie thanked Liam over and over again for a great time.

"It's not over yet," he announced, as he opened the door and grabbed her in his arms. He got her out of her gown in seconds. He dropped his clothes to the floor and was on her urgently.

I could do this for the rest of my life, Charlie thought.

Morning came and Charlie was extremely sore. Her muscles ached from the adventure in the loch. She hoped a long hot shower would help. She still wasn't moving fast and Liam was sweet in packing all their clothing. They had lunch, said their good-byes and headed back home.

They went to his place. "What should we do about dinner?," Charlie asked. "I don't think we have much here. I'll take a walk to the store and pick up a few things. It'll do my muscles some good to be stretched out," she continued. Liam nodded, agreeing with the plan. Charlie didn't feel much like cooking. She was trying to figure out what she could pop in the oven when she saw it - the headline - **Liam's Lady: Made of Honor**

Oh my god! She dipped her head down so no one saw her. Every tabloid had her picture on the front page. Some were of her giving the fisherman mouth to mouth and some had her dragging the guy by the arms on to the shore. She grabbed a pizza and every tabloid there was and ran back to Liam's.

Liam had said this would be a tabloid event.

"Can you believe this?," Charlie yelled, dismayed.

"Yes, I can. What you did was heroic, Charlie."

Opening the articles, there were more pictures of Liam kissing her at midnight and of them dancing. Over all, the tone of the articles was good. They seemed to like her. They had quoted the Chief Medical Officer. There were comments such as 'Has Sir Liam Finally Met His Match?' and 'Blue Blood VS. Blue Collar'. All in all, the press was pro-Charlie.

"I'm going to keep these. I'll send them to my parents"

CHAPTER 22

After several months of the tabloids hounding her and Liam, things did settle down. At least they weren't on the front page every day with pictures of them grocery shopping. The days were getting longer and the weather was slightly improving. Charlie couldn't remember the last time she spent the night at her apartment. She stopped by only to get her mail.

Spring brought with it vacation time. Charlie was impressed by the amount of vacation time allotted here compared to the States. *Five weeks of vacation is a lot!*

Liam was working more than his usual 'Mondays only' schedule. Some days, he was gone before she even awoke and returned home after she was in bed.

Charlie's work was great. Profits had grown by 17% and she had added four more sales representatives. Her profit sharing checks were massive and her stocks were soaring. She was in on all the conference calls linking the three main headquarters every Wednesday. Now Charlie was ready for a break.

"Hi, Jessica. It's Charlie." Charlie called Liam's sister to ask her about vacations. Charlie knew she had to take advantage of the cheap flights and short flight times to mainland Europe. Jessica said she would put together a few ideas and send them over with brochures.

"Hello, Honey" Charlie greeted Liam after his day at work. He answered with a big, huge kiss. Liam was usually a pretty laid-back individual, but it was evident he was stressed.

"Are you OK?" she asked, concerned.

"Things are getting a little crazy at work," he stated.

After a bite to eat, they decided to sit out back. It was dark but not so chilly. They lit a candle and chatted.

"I called Jessica today," Charlie announced, "I have some vacation time coming and I wanted to go somewhere. Are you interested?"

"Sure, make the arrangements where you would like."

She told him of a few of her ideas - Spain, Greece, or perhaps Italy again. He offered up a few suggestions. It was a nice evening but his mind was still on work.

With the weather becoming more agreeable, they made weekend trips up north He always had some charming village in mind for her to discover.

Oban is a few hours drive from Edinburgh and the west coast views are stunning. While they were there, the sun decided not to make an appearance.

Charlie and Liam walked along slowly, holding hands. Neither person said much. Taking in the busy port of this small seaside village, Charlie wondered if those who live in Scotland know how precious their scenery is. The coastlines, the hills, even the architecture evokes a special feeling.

The seagulls squawked while the lines clanked against masts, a constant reminder of the seaside ambiance. The wind whistled through the halyards, producing an eerie sound to match the low gray clouds that cloaked the village, as if, knowing her secret beauty, they were guarding her from the world.

Liam loved hill walking. It was an activity he had enjoyed since his childhood. "It's so peaceful and clears your mind." Liam took pleasure in sharing the stories of the Six Munros he had conquered.

"I couldn't imagine climbing a mountain over 3000 feet, let alone climbing six of them for fun."

No wonder he is in such great shape. After ten minutes, I am panting like a dog for air and he's ready to head for the top.

Oban offered a few smaller hills with spectacular views overlooking Loch Awe. Not so much a challenge for Liam – however to Charlie, these were not hills but mountains. 'The Highlands', Charlie quickly learned, was appropriately named. Standing atop the hill, it all became clear why Liam liked it up here so much.

"I feel like I've conquered the world. I want to jump up and fly with the gulls and scream at the top my voice."

Charlie discovered a new respect for the mountains. After an afternoon of brisk exercise, Liam was invigorated. However, Charlie was worn out.

With steam rising from their soup and the lingering smell of fresh baked bread, they watched from the pub as the boats swayed back and forth on the wind-chopped waters. It was a day to relax and enjoy each other's company instead of focusing on work stress.

"So, Charlie, how did you get the name 'Charlie'?"

"My dad loved silent movies and Charlie Chaplin. He would always talk about the movies from when he was a boy. So, Liam, your favorite 'funny bone' was named after a funny man..........Oh Hell," Charlie cut herself off. The photographers had arrived. *More tabloids. Great. So much for being relaxed.*

Although she tried to appear casual about this intrusion, it was very tiresome making sure she didn't make some etiquette mistake. It really added a lot of pressure to the weekend.

"Lee, how do you handle this?"

"It has been a while since they hounded me this much. After my break up, they were like rats, into everything they could. It's been over a year since they have trailed me. Let's have some fun with them shall we?

Let's hit a jewelry store, the headlines will be all about us getting married."

They both laughed as they set out to have a little fun with the press.

"You know, I could go into one of the little stores and buy a pregnancy test! That would send them over the edge."

"Now you're getting into the spirit!" he gleamed.

April

Jessica sent the travel information she had assembled for the trip to Greece they had discussed. It was as if she had a sixth sense for making arrangements that were perfect for them.

Their trip to Greece was magical. Charlie was uncomfortable that Liam paid for the trip when it was not only a vacation but also Liam's birthday celebration.

"41 years old. How does it feel?"

"I don't feel a day older than when I turned 21, truth be told. I can't hike up the mountains like I used to, but I still make it to the top. And of course, having a younger woman keeps me young at heart." He ribbed clutching his chest.

"You make it sound like I'm a teenager."

"Now there's a birthday wish!" he laughed.

"You're terrible," Charlie said laughing along with him.

They visited all the major islands. The area was steeped in history and Charlie wanted to know and see it all. The sun felt rejuvenating after the cold, dark winter. Charlie was relaxed and there was no threat of paparazzi since Jessica had handled the itinerary. Bathing suit pictures were a big fear for Charlie. The press would have a field day with her physique or excess thereof.

170

Their white cliffside apartment overlooked the sea and the village. The view was breathtaking. The rooftops seemed to be built into the sides of the steep terrain.

Charlie and Liam took long walks holding hands, speaking of dreams and aspirations. They shared childhood stories of learning to ride a bike, first dates and kisses, school and first jobs. Charlie was able to picture his upper class upbringing with the best of everything.

He was going to royal estates for garden parties while she was going to the ocean and riding roller coasters. Their rearing had been very different and yet, even with the differences, their parents had been able to yield two smart, successful, responsible adults who had learned to love and be loved.

"So, you have NEVER been on a roller coaster? I can't imagine. It's such a staple event in a child's life. We'll have to remedy that, perhaps our next trip should be to Disney."

"I'm not sure I am up for a roller coaster at this age! I could make a fool out of myself in so many ways that even thinking about the possibilities makes me cringe."

As they laughed together imagining the tabloid headlines, Charlie thought about if they ever had children. *Guess I would be the one involved in the snowball fights.*

Their relationship was solid. However, they never spoke about the future. That bothered Charlie.

She realized the implications of the relationship. Technically she didn't *live* in Edinburgh; she was there on assignment. Although there was no date set for her to go home, her work permit expired in October. Not that it couldn't be extended, but the fact remained she was a temporary fixture in Scotland.

She had a life and job to return to in Maryland. Her house, her family, all were in the States.

I can't imagine living my life without him. What is going to happen? You can't just say, "Hey that was fun! See ya when I see ya!" I can't do that. You don't find love like this every day.

This was a terrible stress that gnawed at her. She feared the day when decisions would have to be made.

Perhaps that is why this is OK for him? He knows it will end and he is not locked in.

Charlie battled within herself periodically about the subject. She still had a hard time believing sometimes that she could get a man as perfect as Liam. Liam seemed so content. He probably never gave it a thought.

The nights were filled with romantic dinners and passionate escapades. Their room had a private terrace that they used to full advantage. They lay on the soft cushions, gazing at the stars, while a warm breeze danced through their hair. Everything was perfect. No woman could dream of anything more than a man like Liam.

"What are you thinking?" he asked while watching their fingers intertwined together.

Charlie could hardly tell him her true thoughts- *the fear of what was to come.* She didn't want to ruin the Eden she had found.

"I was thinking about how perfect you are. How you make me feel and how my heart skips a beat when you say my name."

Liam began kissing her again. Charlie took note of every muscle movement in his body with her hands.

For the rest of my life, no matter what happens, I will never forget this perfect moment.

Ten days went too quickly. As in Italy, Charlie could have stayed there forever with him. It didn't matter where she went as long as he was there.

172

"Did you have a nice time, Chuck?"

"Of course, besides, I could have a great time anywhere with you. I can't wait to get my pictures developed. I know exactly which one I want to put on my desk. I think I should have written a few more postcards to my friends though."

Upon their return to Edinburgh, Charlie set out on the womanly duties of unpacking, laundry and grocery shopping. Liam immediately tucked himself away in his office to catch up on his work. *Back to the daily grind.*

During the rest of that summer they went away for long weekends on the many bank holidays that Scotland enjoys. Liam never sat still; they always had some place special to go. Charlie was amazed that he took so much time to plan. He always had a surprise in store for her whether it was a boat ride or a show. The trip to London was a total shocker. He had arranged everything she loved from theatre tickets to tours.

His work schedule was still heavy, but he always had time for her. Charlie could tell the stress was taking its toll on him and she loved being supportive. She packed him lunch and cooked hearty breakfasts. She would run a bath for him to relax and made sure he was satisfied in all matters of the bedroom.

"Charlie?" Liam called from his office upstairs.

"Hi, Honey, what's up?" she asked opening the door.

"This weekend a couple of my University polo team mates and I are going to New Castle for a boy's weekend. I will be leaving Friday and I will be home Sunday night. I was wondering if you would want to go down to Livingston and go shopping with my sister or if you want to stay here."

"Well, I think I will stay here if that is OK. Adele wants us to come over for a party she is having Saturday night and Louise got a new cat that I promised I would come and see one of these days."

"All right, so you will you be OK for a couple of days then?" he asked, concerned about being away.

"Of course, I will. Go have fun. You've been working too hard lately; I think this is just what you need."

She gave him a big kiss as she sat on his lap. Liam reached into his desk drawer and handed Charlie a small exquisitely decorated bag.

"This is for you," he began, "because no matter where I am or where you may be, I want to know that I am there with you."

Charlie became incredibly nervous at the thought of what could be in the bag. *Is he acknowledging that we may have to separate? Is this him finally bringing it up? Am I reading too much into this? Open the bag Charlie!*

Inside the bag was a beautiful box. There was no question that it was from a jeweler. *No chance, Charlie, don't even go there, no chance at all that this is THE ring and this is a proposal. Take a breath and come down from that cloud.*

To her astonishment it was a ring, a gorgeous ring. All Charlie could do was stare. The dark blue sapphire sparkled in the light; she had never seen a sapphire this big. The diamonds circling the gem added a contrast, making the stone seem darker and more mysterious.

Then confusion set in. *If this were an engagement ring, there would have been words of marriage. What finger do I put it on? What do I say?*

"Liam, my God, it's amazing. You bought this for me?" she was flabbergasted.

"Yes, my love, for you."

Charlie took the ring out of the box and placed it on her right hand finger. It was a perfect fit. She couldn't take her eyes off of it. *Holy shit!* Her stomach was doing cartwheels, there were show tunes going off in her head.

"I love it! Thank you so much. I don't think I have ever seen anything this gorgeous in my life."

Within minutes, the desk was being utilized in ways for which it had never been intended.

CHAPTER 23

"I can't believe August is finally here! I am so excited to see the Military Tattoo tonight. I think I am more excited than I am for Christmas. My mother will be here in a few days as well." Charlie declared.

"The Tattoo is definitely something to be excited about, no matter how many times you have seen it. It is a tradition of which we Scots are very proud. There is no greater feeling than the one experienced by seeing and hearing the mass pipes and drums engulfing the entire Castle Esplanade. It gives me goose flesh. My favorite part, however, is the very end. When the flag is lowered, a single spot light shines on the Lone Piper, as he stands high on the wall of the Half Moon Battery playing to the awestruck crowd. You get a clear understanding of how powerful the bagpipes can be. It was the military's call into battle. As the young men heard the drones of the pipes they would charge toward their enemy. The pipes to most are a sacred instrument," Liam concluded.

Charlie smiled at his detailed and heartfelt explanation. She was learning that all Scots take the tattoo dead serious – it's regarded like church.

During the whole two-hour program, Charlie was riveted. She sat on the edge of her seat the entire time not wanting to miss one eyeful of the maneuvers or the performers. Liam was caught between watching the show and watching Charlie's reaction. As the Lone Piper appeared, playing Amazing Grace to the Heavens in honor of all the fallen heroes, he saw the tears well up in her eyes. He knew she had felt the force behind the pipes.

"I don't think I have ever experienced anything like that before in my life, Liam." Charlie confessed. "It was awe-inspiring. I really would like to take my mother to see it if it's possible."

"You can understand now why people travel from all over the world to come to Edinburgh to see the Tattoo. I am glad you enjoyed it, Charlie. The Tattoo normally sells out by January, but I will see what I can do about another set of tickets for you and your mother."

Two days later, Charlie set out to the airport to pick up her mother. Marlene Watson was a laugh. She loved her wine and a more social butterfly would never be found. Liam took his two ladies to all the finest places and arranged for wonderful getaways for mother and daughter. Marlene took an instant liking to Liam and had never seen her daughter so happy and content.

While Liam worked, Marlene and Charlie enjoyed the day trips offered by the coach services. They discovered lovely villages, were enchanted by the folklore of the Highlands and toured as many castles as they could possibly visit in the time at hand. Not a stone was left unturned. They took a cruise on Loch Ness in search of Nessie and did their part for the economy with their shopping.

They enjoyed the Edinburgh Festival, seeing show after show, filling their days walking the streets watching all the performers and taking in the bustle of the festival atmosphere.

Liam managed to acquire another set of tickets to the Military Tattoo. Charlie was thrilled to experience it again. It was the highlight of her mother's trip.

"Mom, on Friday we are going to Livingston to have dinner with Liam's family. They are wonderful people but very formal. Charlotte, his mother, is the Grandniece of the Queen, can you get over it!!"

"You love him, don't you?" her mother asked with the excitement of a proud parent.

"I do, Mom. He is wonderful to me."

Marlene couldn't help notice a tinge of sadness in her voice.

"But?" Marlene encouraged.

"But what?" Charlie asked.

"You had a bit of something in your voice. There is either a 'but' or a 'however' in there some where."

Charlie began her confession about her fears. In two months time, she would be facing leaving. She feared how he never spoke of the future other than a weekend trip. Then she explained that somehow he never made her feel as though she was temporary and this caused her confusion.

"It's almost as if he has forgotten I don't live here and I need to remind him!" she cried.

"You've never spoken of it at all?"

"Never. Not one time. The closest he ever got was the ring when he said, 'No matter where you are I want you to know I am with you'. But he was going away for the first time alone since we met, he could have been referencing that for all I know."

Charlie's frustration and dread were easily heard. "Should I say something?" Charlie looked at her mother.

Marlene felt for her child. It was a difficult situation. It wasn't easy to come up with the answer. Truth be told, she didn't have an answer. The plea for help on Charlie's face was painful for Marlene to see. There wasn't a right answer, she concluded. Each option ran it's own risks.

"Charlie, I don't know, Sweetheart. I can see your dilemma. Sometimes doing nothing is the best action to take. At least, if you let it run its course, at some point in time, it won't be able to be ignored. Then you will both have to be on the same page at the same time. Now might be too early for him to think about it. On the other hand, he may be waiting for you to make a move since in reality the ball is in your court. It would be up to you if you stayed. I am sure keeping your job in some capacity is possible. And he may not want to pressure you; he may want you to make the decision on your own."

"Perhaps you're right. I never thought about it that way. All the changes would be on my end and maybe that is why he phrased what he said when he gave me the ring that way. Thanks, Mom. Now I have a new way to look at it. I'll think on that for a while."

The dinner with Liam's family went off without a hitch. Everyone got along extremely well. Charlotte and Marlene talked for hours and when Charlie questioned her mother later on the topics of their discussion, Marlene was vague.

"I hope you weren't up to anything, Mom. I know how you like to get people involved. You are famous for always having a co-conspirator." Mom didn't take the bait. That mystery would remain.

"He has a charming family, very nice people."

The trip was winding down. Charlie was sad her mother would be leaving. It was so nice to have someone else around who knew her and cared for her. Marlene enjoyed Edinburgh and thought it was a wonderful place. In the past two weeks of her visit, she had noticed many changes in her daughter. She was more confident and happy. She did have a glow about her that only love can bring. Marlene was sure the situation would work it's self out.

"Love does conquer all," thought the hopeless romantic.

"Did you enjoy your mother's visit?" Liam asked.

"I wish she could have stayed. It was so nice having her here. The Festival -- I cannot get over how the city is so alive. And there are still two more weeks to go! I wish my dad could have come over too."

"Well, you never know, perhaps next year," he offered.

"I'm not supposed to be here next year." Charlie said with her voice trailing off.

This was the first either of them had spoken out loud about her leaving. Liam passed no comment, but there was an uncomfortable feeling in the air. Charlie was torn between coming out with it and asking him his thoughts on the situation but she was scared of his answer at the same time.

What if he asked you to marry him? What would you do?

She went to bed pondering what it would be like to live in a foreign country forever. But then, there would be the excitement of being Liam's wife. She drifted off to sleep wrapped in the arms of the man she loved, not knowing if in two months time she would even be in the same country with him.

By the end of the Edinburgh Festival, work for Charlie had started to pick up. It was time to add another sales rep because her people were having difficulty keeping up with the new business. Charlie continued to do a lot of work from home in order to stay on top of everything. Roger turned into a major player and assisted in most of the office's daily performance.

He would be able to run the office if I were to leave. Perhaps I should speak with Mr. Moore about Roger's abilities.

By the time September was halfway finished, Charlie was dreading having to speak with Mr. Moore regarding her transition home. She had been putting it off and she still couldn't bring herself to do it. She wasn't ready to leave. The thought of leaving Liam debilitated her. Her heart crashed into her gut when she contemplated it for too long. Charlie pressed forward with work, waiting for Mr. Moore to bring it up.

CHAPTER 24

"Charlie, we have to talk." Liam said brusquely walking in from work.

Charlie did not like his tone. Those words were always followed by bad news. Her heart started pounding immediately.

"I have a grave feeling, I'm not going to like what you are about to say. Should I spare myself all the details and pack my stuff?" she said quite seriously.

"Well, that's going to be up to you. It's my wish that you don't but knowing you, I don't think I'm going to win this one, as I knew from the beginning."

"From the beginning? The beginning of what?" she was shaking.

Liam lowered his head and looked at the floor. His voice quivered with desperation, "I had to Charlie. I was the pawn, not you. All that time you thought I was hesitating because I had been hurt by Isabelle and Rebekah but I was hesitating because I was falling in love with you and I knew this day would come. I decided to ignore what I had to do and enjoy to the fullest what time I had with you. I'm sorry. Even though I know my apology won't matter"

"You had to do what?" her eyes were wide and she stood perfectly still even though she felt her world shattering around her.

"I was supposed to meet you, Charlie. Your firm was cooperating in the investigation. The lead man had several transactions with your firm and we chose your company as the decoy. You were able to help provide me with clues and details we wouldn't have had. I was supposed to help you, be your friend. There was nothing stating I had to fall in love with you, which I did, honestly. I am telling you now because the investigation is complete. The government gave their press release to the papers and it will all be out tomorrow. You would have figured it out in a day or two and I wanted you to hear it from me."

Charlie was gutted. She was in shock. "The whole thing was an investigation," she whispered slowly, realization coming through, "You meant to meet me? You invented our friendship? You pretended?" her voice was barely audible. Liam stood in front of her, thinking only that he was a horrible monster. She walked toward the door and grabbed her purse as she exited. It was raining. It was always raining. Charlie was too numb to notice. She couldn't even cry. She was empty. She couldn't even think.

She went back to her apartment. She had nothing there. Not even something for a cup of tea. Liam had called her cell phone several times. She never answered. *It was all make believe. It was only a part of his job. Imaginary. Made up. Invented. Fabricated. A lie. I was a tool, a mode of information. I was collateral damage.* Charlie stared at the wall unable to feel anything until she fell asleep.

She stayed cocooned in her apartment the next day. She didn't call work. She never uttered a word. She never ate or showered. She sat, continuing to stare at the wall, devoid of all emotion. Incapable of coping, she shut down. Her cell phone was ringing continuously until the battery gave out. Her front door buzzer was constant. She never flinched. For two days, she remained as such. By Friday, she knew she had to go to work. It was the hardest thing she had ever done.

When she walked into her office, Louise was the first to greet her.

"Charlie, I'm so sorry. I've called you and called. Are you ok?"

"Yes, I am perfectly fine. Shit happens." Her tone was not right and the fake smile was not hard to see through. Charlie made it to her office and collapsed in her chair. She tried to concentrate on work. She puttered about with some reports, did payroll, but otherwise she existed.

"Charlie?" Louise called through the speaker, "I have Liam on the line. He's been calling for days"

"I'm in a meeting Louise. I can't take the call now," she replied.

Louise knew it was a lie. After several hours Louise came in. "Charlie, I need to know what you want me to do. The press are calling and coming in. I am sending them away and taking messages. Is there a statement you want me to make?" Louise sincerely was upset for Charlie.

"No, Louise. I think nothing is the best action. Anything I do will be misconstrued and twisted. I think it's best if I do nothing," she conceded. Louise tried to console her friend. Charlie wasn't having it.

"I can handle a breakup. Although, I guess, it was a one sided breakup since there was nothing on Liam's end," Charlie muttered.

"That's not what he's saying to the papers. He is calling you the most incredible woman alive. That he couldn't have been more proud of a living soul than he is of you," Louise enlightened her.

"Well I suppose he has to cover his ass so he doesn't look like a monster," Charlie replied.

Charlie threw herself into her work. She thought about nothing else. She had a company to run and she was going to do it. She pulled herself up and out of it and trudged forward. By the end of the day, she had made significant progress on the work backup.

Leaving for the day, she waltzed past the paparazzi. She walked with her head up and a smile on her face and

184

she went straight home. She walked into her apartment to find six dozen red roses and a card. All of her clothes were there, and her key. She quickly searched her apartment to make sure he was gone. *I'm not sure I want to open the card.* Charlie held the card in her hand for a long while before she had enough guts to open it.

Charlie,
This is not what I want. I love you. I will always love you. I will again apologize for how we began and how it has ended, but I will cherish the middle for the rest of my life.
Forever and Always,
Liam

Charlie still hadn't cried. Even now, in a confession so touching, she was numb. *He still chose to carry on knowing the outcome. He knew the terms and conditions. He had a choice. I didn't. Unforgivable.*
Charlie barely ate. Day after day, she only existed. Not one day was easier than the day before. Work was her saving grace. Weeks went by and the hurt was still there.

The tabloids were having a full-blown affair with the break up. They weren't leaving Charlie in any peace whatsoever. Functioning at work was difficult. The press kept calling and swarming outside the door. Today's headlines took the cake: **Sorry Charlie! There Are Other Fish In The Sea** and **It's Elementary, My Dear Watson.** That article went on to explain why they would never make it due to his blue blood and her blue collar.

Yesterday's headlines were pretty good as well: **Marshall Law: The New Way To Break A Case**, highlighting the facts about Liam being involved the whole time in her company's investigation. Then there was **Love'm And Liam** that fired off all the women in Liam's life. Liam had been calling her regularly but she never answered. After work Charlie would go home and stay there. Adele came over a few times to check on her, as did Louise. But all in all, Charlie became reclusive.

She decided to get out of town. She booked herself into a resort in Malaga. Some time away was what she needed. She sat in the sun and thought about the past year. The vacation together in March, her mother's visit, their sensual love making, she thought it all through. Nothing added up. He had gone through a lot of trouble and expense to gain what exactly? Anything he wanted, he could have had by court subpoena. He had no reason to involve her. What information could he have possibly gained from her? He had access to her computer. There was nothing on it to help. He had access to her office. She was still not sure what that would do.

I am such a fool. I was paraded around in front of all these people who were laughing at me and now they are laughing last.

Charlie hated not getting the final word. She started scheming on how to get back at Liam but her heart wasn't in it. She was crushed, devastated. Broken. She hadn't called her mother or Ally. She couldn't bare it. As it turned out, three days in Spain didn't help one bit.

Every day Liam tried calling her, either on her cell phone or at work. He continued to make sure she didn't forget about him. He sent flowers, candy, even jewelry.

I thought we had the discussion on baubles. Not impressed.

She sent everything back, never even reading the cards. Charlie wished he would go away.

The press weren't letting up either. The closer it came to the trial starting, the more flurried they became. Speculation was all over the papers about whether Charlie would testify. Pictures of Liam with other women already graced several covers. Brutal.

Charlie had lost a significant amount of weight by not eating for several weeks. Her pale complexion and darkly circled eyes had Louise very worried about her. Charlie was working 12-14 hours a day. She was there when Louise arrived each morning and she was still there when Louise left each night. Louise imagined Charlie had her own way of dealing with her issues but she was starting to look unhealthy.

Louise wasn't sure if this was classified as a work situation or a personal one because it did overlap. She considered calling Mr. Moore but it didn't seem the right action to take. Louise even considered calling Liam, but that seemed almost like she was backstabbing her friend. All she could do was watch her friend struggle.

"Charlie, do you want me to pick you up something for lunch?" Louise asked.

"No, I'm fine. I'm not hungry."

"Charlie, you cannot live on coffee. You don't look well. Please let me get you something," She begged her friend.

"Louise really, my God, I am fine. What do you mean I don't look well?" she barked.

"You don't look rested. You look tired and burdened. Why don't I come over tonight and make a slap-up meal and we can talk, whatever you want?"

"Thanks, Louise, but I have so much work to do, I have no idea what time I will get out of here."

She tried, but Louise was running out of options.

Charlie woke up determined to look rested. She had finally slept. Louise was right on that point. Sleep was something Charlie was avoiding. She would lie there and remember all the nights with Liam or replay old tapes in her head of conversations when she should have picked up on his clues. Like at Christmas, "I just want a simple life." It seemed to hold a different meaning looking back on it now. Perhaps he did have a bit of guilt? *Doesn't matter now*, she told herself. She dressed for work. She started to head for her office but she ended up not going.

The courtroom was packed as Charlie sneaked in.

I don't know why I am here. After all, this stupid case ruined my life!

Curiosity had gotten the better of her, and not being one for self-control, here she was. Placing her briefcase at her feet, she looked around to make sure no one noticed her. After all the drama that had played out over the past few weeks someone was bound to recognize her. Then it would get back to Liam that she was there.

I hope he doesn't interpret my being here as support. I hope he loses the damn case.

Charlie had never been to High Court. She was surprised how easy it was to get in.

This was the third day of testimonies and examinations. There was Liam sitting at the front, with papers covering a huge table.

"Mr. Duval, tell me, Sir, how is it that a woman of Ms. Shockley's minimal experience and work history came to draw such a huge salary?" Liam looked powerful and arrogant. He paced the floor before his prey like a hunter. "Explain to me, Sir, the checks she had written to your company."

The line of questioning made Mr. Duval stutter and sweat. He looked terribly nervous. Mr. Duval's coun-

188

selor objected to just about every question Liam was proposing, making him rephrase. The cat and mouse game of verbiage didn't seem to bother Liam in the least. He seemed to enjoy pointing out to the esteemed judges the real question to which he was alluding. There was no jury. Charlie really wasn't sure, even through all the press coverage, what the charges were and against whom. There were a lot of big names and even bigger companies involved. Mr. Duval was but one from Johnston Banks LTD who had gotten mingled in amongst high-rolling players. She didn't know who Ms. Shockley was but the name seemed vaguely familiar. Having thrown herself into work over the past few weeks since their break up, it could have been anywhere that she had seen the name.

Work had been Charlie's retreat. It had been nearly a year since Mr. Duval had been fired and she had assumed his responsibilities. She was privy to most proprietary information and had taken on more and more the role of president/director. Scarcely a word was spoken about a replacement these days and, to Charlie, the more she kept her mind occupied, the better.

She watched him. She could hear her heart beating. The loss she felt was minimal compared to the pain of knowing Liam was no accident. He had planted himself near her and waited for his opportunity. She was preyed upon the same as he was preying on Mr. Duval right now.... A meal for the hungry.

Then Charlie realized that it had been she who had taken the bait. She had gotten her fill. Foreign weekends, grand galas, private lustful moments were all part of a master plan. For Liam it was Work. For Charlie it was Love. Real Love, something she had never felt before. Charlie always believed when it was right, she would know, without a shadow of a doubt, and with Liam she had thought she knew. It was true and forever. She saw her future unfold in front of her night after night as they lay in bed together. It was going to be a good life with Liam.

"Admit it, Mr. Duval, you paid her!" shouted Liam in a voice so thunderous that it snapped Charlie out of her thoughts. Listening intently now to what was unfolding; Liam's questions went from broad to more precise. He had dates, he had times, he had locations, and he had solid reason.

What? Say that again, oh, please, say that again!! Begged Charlie, recognizing what was being asked.

"The property in Oban..." Liam continued.

I know that property. How do I know of that property?

"The £300,000 transfer....." Liam questioned.

That was in May, two years ago.

"In May 2004..."

Yes, yes, I know what he is talking about!! I have to talk to Liam, I know what he is after!!. How do I talk to him? I know what you need. What do I do? How do I get to him?

Frantic, Charlie opened her briefcase and took out her laptop. People looked at her for making so much racket.

I'll have to leave the room but I might miss something I know. I'm not leaving; I'm doing it here.

With a loud beep, her laptop came on and the police were all over her. All courtroom activity halted in that moment and everyone looked at what was taking place. Liam saw Charlie being tethered and hauled from the courtroom.

"Liam, I have what you need!! I know what you're talking about!" Charlie yelled hysterically, "I have it, all of it!!

As the officers continued to struggle to gain control of Charlie, she twisted and thrashed. Charlie never ceased with her outburst. "That's why he broke into my apartment! I have what he was looking for."

She prayed Liam could understand her as the heavy twelve-foot high doors slammed shut.

One officer had her laptop, another her brief case, and two held her.

"Officer, please, I beg you, you have to believe me, I have pertinent information for Mr. Marshall. Please, I need to speak to Liam!" she cried with desperation.

"LIAM," she screamed in the hallway, "LIAM!!"

The farther she was dragged down the hallway, the more she realized what she had done. I'm going to lose my job, I am getting arrested, I am going to be on every tabloid cover there is.

"Please, let me go! I have to speak to Liam. Let me go!! Don't you understand, can't you at least let me explain to you and then you can haul me away! Stop please, please!"

Not one officer spoke or even acknowledged her pleas. Outside the High Court, a police car was waiting with a female officer standing by.

"Ma'am, Please, I beg you. I realized I have all the information..."

"Save it," the officer interrupted, "You can tell everyone all about it when we get to the precinct."

"But I need to tell him...."

"One more word from you and more charges get filed." The female officer was not kind in helping Charlie into the back of the police car. She ended up half lying on the seat.

Charlie went ballistic in the back. "You can't drive away!! Don't you understand?" She was thrashing about like a wild animal screaming at the top of her lungs. Charlie felt the car engine start. Charlie started beating the back of the driver's seat with her feet.

Enraged, the female officer turned to her, "If you kick my seat again, I am going to introduce you to pepper spray, and it's a five minute ride to a shower, if you are lucky!"

"Please," Charlie begged again, "Please, you don't understand. I have to tell him."

"Oh, I understand perfectly. High Court is not a place for you to bring your soap opera!"

Charlie felt the car engaged into gear. "No, you got it all wrong. It's not about...."

"Wait! Tell them not to drive away!" Liam demanded charging out the doors. Charlie, hearing his voice, tried to sit up but couldn't. Her legs were too tangled, so she started kicking the door screaming, "Liam, Liam. I'm in here. I have everything" She screamed louder and kicked harder. "LIAM!!!" The car door finally opened. Charlie felt a shiver of relief.

"Get her out of there," Liam ordered. Hands began pulling on Charlie trying to straighten her contorted body to exit the car; all the while Charlie was yelling crazily, "Liam, I have everything. It's on my computer, get my computer from the officer, I have everything."

Stepping onto the pavement, with the rain pouring down now, Charlie looked up to see her superhero saving her on a cold, rainy day just as he had on the first day they had met. Liam looked at her with pain in his eyes. What pain she wasn't sure, perhaps he had his own regrets.

"I have everything, I have to show you," Charlie stated calmly in a quiet voice.

Her hands were still cuffed behind her back and, strange as it might have seemed, she was thankful for that. She was so happy to see him she couldn't have trusted herself not to throw her arms around him. The handcuffs probably spared her the public humiliation of the newspapers getting a picture of him shrugging her off.

Once the cuffs were removed, Liam took her back inside, briefcase and computer in hand.

"I have one hour," he announced concisely. He was stern. This was business. There was going to be no forthcoming apology or groveling for forgiveness for what he had done. They went into a small chamber and closed the door. *Business it will be then.*

"Don't ask me why I am helping you. I want nothing more than for you to lose this case that you used me for. However, if my company can recoup money, then that is what I want."

Liam offered nothing in reply. Her laptop came on with the same loud beep.

Groping in her briefcase she took out the flash drive.

"I used this at home," her voice quivered at the image flashing in her mind of her cozied up on his couch with a fire burning, "when I worked. I had taken it from a dozen or so that were all hooked together in Mr. Duval's desk. These were the things that he came for when he pushed me that day in the office. He must know now that I have the final one."

Charlie continued, "I didn't know what any of these files were but I saved them in one big folder to look through one day. Every now and then I would open it up and poke around. Until you started asking all those questions, it didn't make much sense to me what they were, but then it all came together."

Opening one file, she started to show Liam scanned receipts and bank slips. Another displayed account numbers. Liam couldn't believe his eyes. It was all there in front of him, every name, every transaction. The records were impeccable.

"Have fun," and with that Charlie walked out of the small chamber. She continued down the long hallway

193

and out of the building. Once outside, the press immediately greeted her.

"Miss, what information did you have? How did you get the information? Where did you get it?"

Charlie kept walking, pushing her way through the deluge of microphones, cameras and other media. It was pouring down rain, fitting for her mood. She was proud of the fact that she had kept her cool in front of the press.

There, I did my bit for justice.

CHAPTER 25

Charlie was in her apartment. She didn't dare go back to work. Lord knows what repercussions waited for her there. It had been five weeks since she had seen Liam before today. He looked tired, once she saw him close up.

Good, I hope he can't sleep a wink out of guilt.

No matter how Charlie rationalized it, Liam waltzed out the victor. He got his man, he got the case, and he got the girl. He got everything he had started out for.

I should have just gotten a cat.

Charlie had lived through some rough days since she had come to Edinburgh but this one was the topper. She had three cigarettes left and she had only bought the pack six hours ago. Her mind was spinning. She should really call Mr. Moore and tell him what happened. She should check into the office before it closed, at least give Louise a call.

She had no idea if the press was still outside her stair door. It had to be all over the news by now. However, Charlie didn't have the strength to confront anyone or anything else today.

She reflected back to the day she arrived in Scotland. She had felt the odds were overwhelming that she would make it here. But she did. *It's a shame,* she thought, *that it has to end like this.* She would have to go back home to nothing. She would be looking for a job most likely and perhaps there were criminal ramifications she wasn't even aware of. All over a man she was never supposed to have met anyway. She would have been better off failing on her own accord in the beginning than being ruined. Shame filled her body.

The tap at the door scared her. *The press! How did they get up here, surely none of my neighbors would have let them in.*

"Who is it?" she asked, annoyed.

"It's me." The answer came simply stated.

"What do you want? You got all you needed. You hit the jackpot today. You don't need me for anything else!" Charlie growled through the door.

But Liam started tapping the door incessantly. Charlie walked back into the living room, closing the hall door behind her. The tapping became louder.

"Charlie," he called out, "You're a hero! Please open the door."

Charlie sat listening to Liam's appeals. Finally, she gave in. "You're gonna get me kicked out of my *flat*! It's bad enough I probably lost my job!" She slammed the door behind him as she walked directly back into the living room.

"Christ, Chuck, how many cigarettes have you smoked? The place is in a shroud." He opened the window. With that she lit another.

"Say what you have to say and be gone. I've paid enough of a price in your charade than to have you here gloating that you won at my expense. You've taken everything from me. I have nothing left you could possibly need."

Liam stared at her. He was a horrible human being. All the pain he had caused her. He couldn't fix it. Her super hero and he couldn't fix what he had done himself. He stood there silent in his own remorse.

"You're a hero, Charlie. The press is calling you the Courtroom Caroler. Because of you, we were able to prove that everyone involved swindled the government out of millions. Their arms reached to many countries and there are other governments involved. This is huge. This case went beyond embezzlement and money laundering. This is treason and all sorts of other terms I won't bore you with. You'll be a national hero when this is over, which is going to be a long while"

"It's already over for me. Like most heroes, I guess, I paid a huge price. Congratulations. Will that be all?"

"No."

"NO?" Charlie asked disgusted." What? You need me to testify? Do you want me to wrap the whole case up for you in a little red bow and put your name on it and sign it from Santa Claus? Get out!"

"No" Liam answered evenly, "I won't go. I love you, Charlie. These last few weeks have been hell for me too. I may have started out with a plan to befriend you but I had no plan on falling in love with you. Every moment I spent in your company made me want to be with you more. I want to be with you for the rest of my life. I had no choice in the matter, Charlie. I was trapped. Marry me!"

"Are you kidding? You would go so far as to *propose marriage* to get what more information you need? You are sick, Liam, absolutely sick. I never want to lay eyes on you again. Get out of here and if you come here again I will call the cops! So help me God. Get out of here now!"

"No! I won't go! I don't need any more information. I have everything I need... except you. I want you. Forget the case. I need you."

"You lied to me, Liam. You led me down the garden path and I fell for it hook, line, and sinker. I can't recover from that. I was feeling honest emotions and you were trying to win an Oscar. I can never trust you again. The person I thought you were doesn't exist. You're a fraud!"

"It wasn't a lie how I felt. Everything we did, everywhere we went, I wanted to be there with you. I kept trying to figure out how I could get out of this without you knowing about it, so we wouldn't be screaming at each other like we are today. I knew what I would lose if you found out and I didn't want to lose you. I wasn't willing to come clean because I knew there was no way to explain it that you would understand. I don't know what else to say. I love you. Honestly, I love you more than anything in the world."

"Get out"

For once, Liam was defeated in a case he could barely plead. He knew there was no way around it. Liam walked to the door and let himself out. He stood on the other side of the door for several minutes listening to Charlie's sobs. All he wanted to do was to console her and tell her everything would be all right, that they would have a great life together till the end of time.

He would have to come up with something. After all, he was her superhero.

CHAPTER 26

Charlie had cried all the tears her body could produce since Liam had left a few hours ago. She was emotionally exhausted. She began making plans to pack her things and to arrange getting back home to Maryland. It was overwhelming.

Charlie's cell phone rang with an unpublished number. She wasn't sure if she should answer. She decided to answer but it was too late. The call rang off and one missed call appeared on her screen.

They'll leave a message. To her surprise, the phone went off again, unpublished number,

" Hello?"

"Charlie, my annointed saint!! You are magnificent!" Mr. Moore's words were so shocking to her that she was speechless.

"What?"

"I read all about it on the internet. It's all over the news. **The Courtroom Caroler Stuns Great Britain With The Facts.**"

"How did you know I was the Courtroom Caroler?"

"I got a phone call from a Liam Marshall. He said he was your close personal friend and the lawyer working the case. He said if it hadn't been for you, he would definitely have lost the case. He said because of you, Johnston Banks stands to recoup millions, that you knew from the beginning that Mr. Duval's reappearance that day almost a year ago spoke volumes. I don't know how to thank you more. You have saved our company from ruin. I'm going to fly out in a few days and we will meet and discuss the future."

"What future? I thought my time here was ending soon. I am ready to come home. There has to be someone groomed enough to be director by now."

"There is, Charlie...YOU."

"ME? But I..."

"Don't worry, we will work it all out. You are a hero. I never questioned that sending you to Edinburgh was the greatest decision I ever made."

"So you knew? You knew you were going to fire Mr. Duval? YOU KNEW?"

"Yes, I knew. We had been working with several authorities regarding the situation. The investigation had already been underway for some time.

But we will discuss it all very soon. Congratulations on your new promotion. I'll have all the salary details etc for you when I arrive. And by the way, for what it's worth, I had been working closest with Liam. He is a good man, no matter what happened, he was stuck between a rock and a hard place. He couldn't jeopardize what the government had set in place for him. He had to stay his course or he would have blown it for the world, as you uncovered."

"You know Liam?" she whispered mystified.

"Yes, I do, and proud to say so. I will call you with my itinerary. Get some sleep, take a few days off, you've earned it. I'll call Louise and take care of everything. Bye for now, Charlie; good job yet again."

It was several minutes later before Charlie actually placed the phone down.

He had no choice. It wasn't his call to tell her. He had to stick with the plan. Charlie was stunned by the phone call. *I'm the new director. I am a director of a company, a worldwide company.*

It was late. The clock on her phone said 1:53AM. Charlie put on shoes and a jacket. She grabbed her keys

200

and walked out the door. It was misting. The air smelled fresh and clean. The paparazzi were gone. She felt a smile coming on the corner of her lips. She walked and she knew exactly where she was going.

Charlie rang the doorbell over and over.

"Get up!! I'm soaked"

The walk to Morningside had cleared her head of a lot of questions. Finally, she saw through the door that a light had just turned on in the hallway. Liam came down the steps dressed in his robe and nearly burst through the door when he saw her there. He grabbed her, hugged her, and kissed her.

"I love you Charlie, I love you! I want you with me forever."

"I love you too, Liam."

Wrapped up tight in Liam's arms, she thought, *I could do this for the rest of my life.*

EPILOGUE

Charlie heard the words echoing through her head as the priest proclaimed to the congregation, "I now present to you Mr. and Mrs. Liam Marshall." It was as if the clock stopped ticking and for a whole minute the world was hers to see as she wished it. The church was filled with faces – some familiar, most not. There was no sound and there was no movement. Everyone and everything was frozen as if she was taking a mental still-frame picture. It was all too much to experience.

"Are you ok?"
"I am. I am absolutely fine!" She smiled up at her husband.

While standing before the whole of the congregation, Charlie watched Charlotte Montgomery Marshall rise from her pew and walk toward them. She climbed the three small steps to stand before Charlie and Liam.

"Liam, my only son, you have made a worthy choice." Removing her Marshall plaid from around her neck, Charlotte draped the tartan over Charlie's shoulder and kissed her on each cheek.

"Welcome to our family."

Cheers erupted from the wedding guests.

The Mail's headline read:

FOR THE REST OF THEIR LIVES

ORDERING INFORMATION

To order additional copies of
For The Rest Of My Life
contact lindenhill2@comcast.net

Linden Hill Publishing also has a wide se-
lection of books available that can be ordered on line on our secure server. Learn
more about these books on the website.
www.lindenhill.net